ALSO BY

AMARA LAKHOUS

Clash of Civilizations
Over an Elevator in Piazza Vittorio

DIVORCE ISLAMIC STYLE

Amara Lakhous

DIVORCE ISLAMIC STYLE

*Translated from the Italian
by Ann Goldstein*

Europa
editions

Europa Editions
214 West 29th Street
New York, N.Y. 10001
www.europaeditions.com
info@europaeditions.com

Translation by Ann Goldstein
Original title: *Divorzio all'islamica a viale Marconi*
Translation copyright © 2012 by Europa Editions

Library of Congress Cataloging in Publication Data is available
ISBN 978-1-60945-066-3

Lakhous, Amara
Divorce Islamic Style

Book design by Emanuele Ragnisco
www.mekkanografici.com

Cover illustration by Chiara Carrer

Prepress by Grafica Punto Print – Rome

Printed in the USA

To Vito Riviello (1933-2009)
A great poet and a dear friend

Since love and fear can scarcely exist together,
if we must choose between them,
it is much safer to be feared than loved.
—NICCOLÒ MACHIAVELLI

As for my irony, or, if we prefer, my satire,
I think it frees me from everything that irritates me,
oppresses me, offends me,
makes me feel uneasy in society.
—ENNIO FLAIANO

DIVORCE ISLAMIC STYLE

ISSA

Finally, on a Saturday afternoon in the last week of April, I become operative. I take the 780 bus from Piazza Venezia and get off at Piazza della Radio. I walk to Piazza Enrico Fermi. There are too many cars—it would take a small miracle to find a parking place. The sidewalks are congested. People are drawn to the clothing stores like flies to honey or garbage.

I stop in front of a display window to stare at the reflection of my face. I'm struck by one detail: the mustache. It's the first time in my life I've grown one, and I seem at least five years older. I've had my hair almost all shaved off, like a marine. For sure I'll save on shampoo and gel! I got some cheap clothes, jeans and a sweater made in China, sending my usual look to hell. In other words, I'm unrecognizable.

For the umpteenth time I stick my right hand into the inside pocket of my jacket. No panic: the wallet's there. But what's happening to me? Am I afraid of being robbed like some tourist? Don't be ridiculous. I just want to reassure myself that I haven't lost my new identity papers—without the residency permit I'm an illegal immigrant at risk of expulsion. By now I've memorized all the new biographical facts. Starting today I have a new name, a new date of birth, a new citizenship, and I was born in a different country.

It takes me a little time to get into character. Meanwhile, I have to get used to this crummy mustache. I have the strange sensation of being inside someone else's body, an intruder in my own skin. In fact, in Rome I really am a foreigner, it's a city

I don't know well. I must have been here a dozen times, but always passing through. The first time, I came on a class trip. I know it as a tourist, no more or less. Of course, I can boast of having seen the Colosseum, the Trevi Fountain, Piazza Navona, Villa Borghese—just like millions of other people in the world.

And then I shouldn't complain too much; feeling like a foreigner at this particular moment isn't a handicap, in fact it's a great advantage in playing my role. Of course, I don't mean a role in a film—I'm on a dangerous mission. And I have no intention of playing James Bond or Donnie Brasco—I don't have the physique for it.

I stroll around aimlessly for a good hour and a half, back and forth along Piazza della Radio and the Marconi bridge. I want to get familiar with the neighborhood right away. I observe the façades of the buildings attentively—the variety is impressive, like the faces of the people I pass. There are all types: young Africans and Asians selling counterfeit goods on the sidewalks, Arab children walking with father and veiled mother, Gypsy women in long skirts begging. In other words, I'm in the Italy of the future, as the sociologists say!

In these circumstances I'm like an animal in search of a new habitat. You have to conquer the territory with your teeth. I'm not greedy, I just want a little place in the shelter of Viale Marconi. Am I asking a lot? I don't think so. I decide to go on the attack, like a tiger that has to feed its pups. The warmup phase has already lasted too long; I have to enter the game.

I leave Piazza Fermi and take Via Grimaldi to my destination. Now I'm in front of the call center. I glance at the big letters over the entrance: Little Cairo. O.K., here we are! I take a deep breath and enter resolutely, launching the first Arabic words of the day.

"*Assalamu aleikum!*"

"*Aleikum salam!*"

A fellow named Akram, whom I've seen in photographs

taken in Mecca, responds. Akram is the owner of the place, as well as suspect No. 1. It's likely that he's the head of the first cell. He's fifty, a bit chubby, wears an elegant white shirt. With sideburns, and a hat, glasses, and black shoes and pants, he'd resemble the legendary John Belushi. Like every good merchant he has a broad smile stamped across his face. You have to communicate trust and positiveness. Clients are like children, they always need to be coddled and reassured. On the wall at the left, high up, in the corner near the ceiling, is a television. It's five, time for the news from Al Jazeera. There are at least four young Arab guys staring at the screen who look like they don't want to be disturbed for any reason whatever. It's not impossible that Osama bin Laden could appear in person to hurl new threats against the West.

I ask Akram if I can make a call to Tunisia. He nods his head yes and invites me with a finger to choose a booth (he can't speak; he, too, is focused on Al Jazeera). Without thinking I choose No. 3, my lucky number. Captain Judas (I'll talk about him later) provided me with a couple of numbers in Tunisia I can use that won't rouse suspicions. Who am I going to be talking to? What will I say? I have no idea. It's a real mystery.

I feel like an actor in a play who has to perform without a script. I have to improvise, I have no other choice. I dial the first number, it's ringing. After ten seconds a woman's voice answers and asks who's calling. I have an instant of hesitation, then I say, "It's Issa." And she: "*Wildi ya kebdi!* My son, my little chick."

Surprise No. 1: I have a second affectionate mother, who speaks Tunisian like me!

The conversation lasts ten minutes. We talk about this and that, from the health problems of the "grandparents" to "papa's" business, from the latest news of "brothers" and "sisters" to changes in the weather.

Surprise No. 2: I have a nice big family, even the grandparents are still living! The end of the phone call is really moving, the list of instructions from an affectionate Tunisian mamma to her émigré mamma's boy: "Don't catch cold, don't forget your Arabic, don't trust women in general and European women in particular, don't drink alcohol, don't go around with hoodlums, don't get into debt."

I hang up and go to pay. I wait a bit, Akram is busy with two other clients. When my turn arrives I take out my wallet and give him a ten-euro bill. I add in a neutral tone that I made a call to Tunisia: I want everyone to know I'm Tunisian.

Akram, however, doesn't give a shit about my country of origin. He looks at his idiot computer, where the cost of the calls is indicated, gives me seven euros in change, and goodbye and thanks. He wants to get rid of me like that, without even knowing who the fuck I am! No, I'm sorry, but that's not for me. Friend, I'm not asking you to invite me to dinner at your house or go to a café and drink tea with me, but at least give me the chance to introduce myself properly. It costs you nothing. Am I a new client or not? Don't I deserve a little respect? You're a businessman, you should know that the client is always and everywhere king! Instead of going away disappointed and defeated I stand fixed to my spot.

"Can I help you with something else, brother?"

"Yes."

That damn yes! I don't know what to say! I have to invent something in a hurry. There's the risk of looking like an idiot with Judas, who wants results, right away, and keeps repeating, like a parrot: "We're playing in the Cesarini zone." In other words, there's no time to waste, the game is about to end.

Luckily, in extremis I get an idea.

"Could you make two copies of my residency permit, please?"

"Of course."

Obstacle overcome. Luckily, I can continue. Before returning the document, Akram gives an extended glance, I would say exaggerated, to the contents. He doesn't seem embarrassed. Ever heard of that shit thing called privacy? He has the look of a border patrol agent. Over the years I've seen plenty of these lousy cops at the airport!

I make the first move to break the ice.

"Don't tell me it's counterfeit."

"No, it doesn't seem so. I was looking at the address. You live in Palermo?"

"I did live there, not now. I moved to Rome a while ago."

"You escaped Sicily because of the Mafia, eh?"

"You're right, I really did escape, but because of the unemployment. Now I'm looking for a place to sleep and a job."

"May God help you."

"Amen."

"My name is Akram, I'm the owner of the shop."

"Nice to meet you. My name is Issa."

"See you soon, inshallah."

"Inshallah."

My dear Akram, you'll have me underfoot a lot in the coming days, God willing, or, rather, inshallah. It's a promise I'll keep. You can be sure.

After the introductions I feel calmer. I can take home the first results. I've made an appearance at Little Cairo. Nothing exceptional—no comparison with the Madonna's appearance to the three children of Fatima. You have to keep your feet on the ground. The important thing is to avoid false moves or irreversible mistakes. And yet I can't help thinking of what Akram said about Sicily. Will we ever manage to get rid of this Mafia label? The outlook isn't good.

I was right not to talk too much to the Egyptian alias John Belushi. Judas urged me strongly not to be too friendly right away. There will be other occasions for socializing. Better not to be in a hurry, someone might get suspicious. Or, worse, I could inspire hostility at the first meeting, and after that everything would be more complicated.

I have to constantly remind myself that I'm Tunisian, and this neighborhood is full of Egyptians. Many people don't know that there are rivalries among the Arabs. For example, it's not smooth sailing between Syrians and Lebanese, between Iraqis and Kuwaitis, between Saudis and Yemenis, and so on and so on. It's why they can't seem to come up with a plan for unity, in spite of a common history, geography, Arabic, Islam, and oil. The model of the European Union will have to wait!

I leave Little Cairo and walk to the 170 stop on Viale Marconi. When the bus comes I find a seat near the window. As it heads toward Termini station I begin to reflect on the mission: was I right to say yes? Can I still abandon it? Will I measure up? Goddamn performance anxiety. I'm confused and a little agitated. Thoughts and memories surface without warning. I try to concentrate. I don't know why, but my grandfather Leonardo comes to mind. We were really fond of each another. When I was small we'd sit looking at the sea, in Mazara del Vallo. He would tell stories and I'd listen for hours without ever getting bored.

He had enough stories to fill a stack of books. He was born in Tunis to a family of immigrants from Trapani. He had lived there until adolescence, before returning to Italy. In the last years of his life he wanted desperately to see the city of his birth. I would have liked to go with him. Sadly, he had heart trouble, so it didn't seem like a good idea to revive those strong emotions, he wouldn't have held up. And yet maybe what he wanted was in fact to be carried away by those emotions—to die and be buried in Tunis, beside his mother.

My grandfather was a splendid person. His stories were never melancholy; he always managed to avoid nostalgia, "the brute beast," he called it. He wept only once, remembering his mother, who died when he was a child. It was he who taught me my first words in Tunisian Arabic: *Shismek*, what's your name? *Shniahwelek*, how are you? *Win meshi*, where are you going? *Yezzi*, enough? *Nhebbek barsha*, I love you very much. And a lot of others.

In Mazara I grew up with the children of the Tunisian fishermen. We were always together, playing, fighting, and immediately making peace. I was often taken for one of them: I had typically Mediterranean features and I spoke Tunisian Arabic well.

I visited Tunis for the first time when I was thirteen, with my family. We took the boat in the late afternoon and arrived at the port of Tunis early the next morning. That night I couldn't sleep, I was so excited. We stayed for two weeks. It was an unforgettable journey for me: I finally saw the land where my grandparents were born. Since then I've been back several times.

After high school, no one was surprised when I decided to enroll in the faculty of Oriental languages at the University of Palermo. I wanted to improve my Arabic. At the university I began studying classical Arabic; I was determined but also enthusiastic. I really liked the grammar, which drove everyone else crazy, not just the students but the professors. I was one of the best students, and a lot of people couldn't believe that my native language was Italian.

I wrote my thesis on Giuseppe Garibaldi's sojourn in Tunisia. The research was very difficult—I don't know why I like complicated things so much! What does Garibaldi have to do with Tunisia, you ask? He does have something to do with it, he does. The Hero of the Two Worlds arrives in Tunis in 1834 to escape the death sentence for insurrection pronounced by the court in Genoa. He spends a year in the Tunisian capital under the false name of Giuseppe Pane, working for the Bey of Tunis. After that, he continues his adventures as a revolutionary in Brazil, where he supports the independence movements against the Portuguese and the Spanish. In 1859, he returns to Tunis, but the authorities deny him entrance when the French consul intervenes. For his local admirers Garibaldi continues to be a hero, a true revolutionary. For his detractors, on the other hand, he is merely an outlaw, a dangerous terrorist.

After I got my degree I often went to Tunisia, and I also had opportunites to visit other Arab countries: Algeria, Morocco, Yemen, Jordan, Egypt, Lebanon, Syria. Obviously, people often continued to take me for a Tunisian, but I didn't mind at all.

I would have liked to have an academic career, but a flunky no—I really didn't want to be the professor's servant and kiss his ass. I took several exams so I could study for a doctorate, but without getting anywhere. I quickly understood that the system was of the Mafioso type, with all kinds of godfathers, bosses, and affiliates. In other words there was nothing left for me. So I was satisfied with a job at the court in Palermo as an Arabic interpreter. Luckily, or unluckily, there are a lot of Arab criminals (mostly from the Maghreb), and percentagewise they have a large presence in Italian prisons. So there was never any shortage of work. Then Captain Judas arrived to turn my life upside down.

It all began a few weeks ago.

I was coming out of the courtroom during the lunch break when a guy in a gray suit came up to me; he was around forty, tall and lean. Right away I thought he was a new judge or a lawyer on a business trip.

He said to me in a serious tone:

"Signor Christian Mazzari?"

"Yes."

"Hello. I'm Captain Tassarotti from the SISMI, military intelligence. I'd like to talk to you."

The word "SISMI" didn't scare me. In three years of work at the court it often happened that I worked with the antiterrorism squad. In particular I'd been asked to translate telephone wiretaps and propaganda flyers.

Together we left the court. We got into a waiting car, and the driver immediately headed toward the sea.

The captain's way of proceeding impressed me. He got to the point immediately, without beating around the bush; maybe he was in a hurry or maybe he had intuited my great need for coffee in order not to fall asleep. He started off with a sentence that left no room for doubts: "Signor Mazzari, we need you for a mission."

He took a piece of paper from a file and asked me to read it carefully. I noted that the document, printed on letterhead and marked by various stamps, had many blacked-out lines. The letters, however, appeared to have been written on a typewriter.

Subject: Operation Little Cairo

Our services have received reliable information from American and Egyptian colleagues, according to whom a large-scale attack is being planned in Rome. Two terrorist cells seem to be involved in the operation. ███████ up to now we have succeeded in identifying only one of them.

The subjects gravitate around Little Cairo, a call center in the Marconi neighborhood. The place is managed by an Egyptian citizen, ███████, and frequented by many foreigners, especially Muslims.

This information confirms the contention of the Western intelligence services that Al Qaeda has changed its strategy with respect to September 11th. Today it no longer relies on terrorists arriving for a mission but is taking advantage of the presence of Muslim immigrants in the West to commit attacks.

The attacks of March 11, 2004, in Madrid fit into this

new criminal design: the terrorist Jamal Zougam and his accomplices were for the most part Moroccan immigrants, apparently integrated into Spanish society.

██
██
██████████████████████████████████

We are obliged to use all possible means to defend ourselves from these new terrorists "made in Italy." In the current situation we do not have sufficient operatives available to evaluate the structure and modus operandi of this terrorist group. ████████████████████

There are numerous questions: are the two cells in question autonomous or affiliated with some international terrorist organization like Al Qaeda? What are the perceptible objectives chosen in order to strike Rome, capital of the Italian State and home of the Vatican? ███████████████
██
██
████████████████████████ab.

Yet we have known for a while that they have targeted: the Colosseum, the Jewish ghetto, the Basilica of St. Peter, the Termini station, the subway, and the United States Embassy on Via Veneto.

██
██
████████████████████

It's likely that the first cell on Viale Marconi functions as a cover, that is, providing logistical support to the other. It is suspected besides that there are suicide bombers ready to act to cause the maximum number of victims. For this reason an emergency plan must be put in place under which help can be provided to thousands of wounded. In the light of all this, we consider it indispensable to prepare public opinion for the worst, at the risk of causing alarm.

At present we are working to identify the elements of the second cell. To accelerate the time frame of Operation Little Cairo, we have decided to ███████████████

██
██
██████████████████████████████.

Rome, April 21, 2005

I didn't need any more details; the official from SISMI had the answers to all the questions that occurred to me. So, after a few minutes, I knew about the mission: I was to be a spy, infiltrated into the Arab Muslim community in Rome, with the purpose of preventing terrifying attacks and saving many human lives.

This captain of the 007s repeated several times that there would be no risk to my safety, because the operation would take place not in the enemy's camp but at home, in Rome. "Signor Mazzari," he said, "don't worry, we will always be nearby."

At the end of the conversation he gave me just a few days to make a decision. When we said goodbye he shook my hand firmly.

"Signor Mazzari, remember that Italy, your country, needs you. We are at war, a war against terror, the 'War on Terror,' as our American allies say."

Shit, "country" and "war" are loaded words! And what was I supposed to do? Feel like the savior of the nation, a modern-day Garibaldi? To tell the truth, the word "country" gives me shivers only when I hear the national anthem at international matches; outside a soccer game I have trouble understanding the meaning of it. It's banal, I know, but it's the truth. Maybe in our imagination it's hard to detach "country" from "war"— like Benito Mussolini, just to be clear.

SOFIA

When you're born you find a name ready and waiting for you: "Peek-a-boo, here I am, see me? I'm your name! Thank you!" Now, let's say that the name you've been given is, for example, Karim or Gamil ("generous" or "handsome," for a boy), or Karima or Gamila ("generous" or "pretty" for a girl). So far, everything goes smoothly, no problem.

Growing up, however, you realize that the name you find pasted onto you in no way matches your character or your looks, because maybe over time you've gotten stingy, or ugly. An insoluble conflict, or, rather, an incurable wound. You can't be generous and stingy, beautiful and ugly at the same time. And so? So nothing. The name becomes a burden to carry on your conscience your whole life. For a lot of people it's a real cross to bear.

No one can choose his own name, I mean first name. Let's say right away that it's not a tragedy; there are worse things in life, like children dying of hunger or women raped in wars. But for an immigrant the question of the name is fundamental.

The first question you're asked is: what is your name? if you have a foreign name it immediately creates a barrier, an impassable boundary between "us" and "you." The name says loud and clear whether you're inside or outside, whether you belong to "us" or to "you." An example? If you live on Viale Marconi and your name is Mohammed it automatically means that you're not a Christian or a Jew but a Muslim. Right? Very likely you're not even Italian because your parents aren't. And so? So nothing. It doesn't count if you were born in Italy, are an Italian citizen, speak Italian perfectly and so on. My dear Mohammed, in the eyes of others you are not (and never will be) a purebred Italian, Italian a hundred percent, thoroughly Italian. Let's say the name is the first indication that we're different.

There are always some clever types who choose a pseudonym, but, unfortunately, the problem is more complex, and can't be resolved that way. It's like putting on a mask to hide your face. Lying to others and above all to yourself doesn't lead anywhere. Lies just don't get very far. Sooner or later the mask falls and the truth is on the surface. It will happen the day you go to the records office to apply for a certificate. And who will you find waiting for you there? Guess. Your original name! It's no coincidence—this meeting was scheduled long ago. And it will be enough to ruin the rest of the day. But if someone really insists on having a pseudonym, I say, no irony intended: please, help yourself!

In my humble opinion, parents shouldn't be in a hurry to give names to their children haphazardly, they should wait until the child grows up and get an idea of his or her character, physical appearance, and so on. You pay dearly for a wrong, inadequate, improvised name, because it produces complexes. Tell me your name and I'll tell you who you are and if you've got any psychological problems. Clear?

Often the name hides the parents' frustrations. Every name has a story. In my case, Safia was chosen by my father without consulting anyone. Poor papa, he expected a boy and had a name ready: Saad, which in Arabic means "auspicious." Before me, my mother had had two girls. With my birth the family had hoped for a shift, a reversal, a radical change, a biological revolution. The family motto was: a boy now! Unfortunately, desire is one thing, reality another.

Saad is a beloved name in Egypt. It recalls our great national hero Saad Zaghloul. Let's say, like George Washington for Americans and Giuseppe Garibaldi for Italians. When my mother was pregnant with me, my father thought of nothing but his future heir, little Saad. My birth took everyone by surprise, throwing many people into despair, my father foremost. A newborn, and already I felt guilty. So I dedicated my first tears to my family. It was painful to see them in such a sorry state.

In other words, the situation was critical. Our family's last name was in danger of disappearing, like a species of bird on the way to extinction. And was I partly responsible for this, or not? Their misery could be read in their faces. It's not right: three girls, one after the other, without a break.

And yet I have to be grateful to everyone (God first of all) not to have been born in pre-Islamic Arabia. Before the Prophet Mohammed, the Arabs buried poor newborn girls alive. What? It's true, really. I swear on the head of my daughter, Aida. Why did they do it? The reasons were ridiculous, utterly illogical.

My father, in a burst of pride and defiance, decided not to betray his political idol. He said to all the relatives who came to see the newborn, "This baby will be named Safia, like the wife of the great Saad Zaghloul." Some consolation! Obviously I couldn't say no.

Having a name like that is no joke. There are a lot of expectations. Performance anxiety is inevitable. Safia Zaghloul was called Umm al-Masriyin, Mother of the Egyptians. She was very involved in social issues, for example the education of girls. In history books she is recalled as the first Arab woman to publicly remove her veil. Also, she took part in the revolution of 1919 against the British occupation.

The name of Safia Zaghloul is often cited because of the role she played in her husband's life, and to illustrate the famous saying that in Arabic goes: "*Waraa kull rajul adhim imraa,"* behind every great man there is always a woman. I've never completely understood what it means. I find it extremely ambiguous; it can be interpreted in different ways. To whom does the term "woman" refer? Grandmother, mother, daughter, wife, granddaughter, lover? And also: a woman who hides behind a man raises some suspicions: why doesn't she go in front? What is she plotting? Does she want to stick a knife in the poor man's back? Is she a coward? Or maybe just timid?

This is the short story of my real name, Safia. But ever since I've lived in Rome I've had another name: Sofia. Let me be clear: it's not a pseudonym, in the sense that I didn't go and look for it. It was given to me and I accepted it. Isn't there a saying, in fact, don't look a gift horse in the mouth?

Why am I called that? I'm not entirely sure. Let's say there are two hypotheses. First: people easily mistake (and without any malice) Safia for Sofia.

"Hi, what's your name?"

"Safia."

"Sofia! What a lovely name."

It's annoying to act like a teacher who corrects her pupils and is quick to clarify: "It's Safia, not Sofia." And then why take offense and make a scene.

Second hypothesis. For many knowledgeable Italians, I (without the veil) look a lot like a famous Italian actress.

"Hi, what's your name?"

"Safia."

"Sofia! Congratulations, you have a great name."

"Thank you."

"You know who you look like?"

"Who?"

"Sophia Loren."

To tell the truth, Sofia is a name I really like a lot. Sofia Loren is a very beautiful woman and I'm fascinated by her story. She was a girl who was born into poverty and became a movie star. Of course, there are always envious people who say nasty things about her. Like that she married a big producer to help her career. The truth is that Sophia Loren is a great dreamer, and I'm like her. What meaning is there in life if you don't have dreams? None. Having a dream to fulfill is the best reason for living. There are people who consider life a real curse, not a gift from God. What a shame! Because in spite of everything life is beautiful.

I don't recall the exact year, but I couldn't have been more than twelve. At that time we lived in Sayyeda Zeineb, a working-class neighborhood of Cairo. One summer afternoon Faten came over; besides being my cousin she was also my best friend. She was very agitated, and was hiding something under her shirt. She looked like someone who'd just left a department store with some intimate lingerie she'd stolen. "Close that door right away," she said. "I have to show you something." She pulled out a foreign women's magazine full of glossy color photographs and in a disdainful tone yelled, "There's your Marilyn Monroe!"

I glanced quickly at the photos and answered, in astonishment, "What do you mean? That's not Marilyn. It looks sort of like her, but don't you see that girl's a brunette?"

"Exactly, Marilyn has dark hair, like us, get it?"

The pictures showed a very young Marilyn, before she became a famous actress. She was pretty, but she wasn't beautiful—in other words, she wasn't Marilyn with the golden hair, whom the whole world is still crazy about.

I was upset and disappointed. But it turned out to be not such a big deal, because a few years later I made a grand discovery: blondes are made, not born! Justice is done! Anyway, the difference between the two Marilyns, the blonde and the brunette, was obvious. There was no doubt about it. Marilyn was beautiful because she had blond hair. And so I began to take very seriously the Arabic saying that half of a woman's beauty is her hair. In Italy they say, instead, *Altezza mezza bellezza*—half of a woman's beauty is her height. Frankly I'm not so sure. Why? Imagine a pair of lovers walking in the center of Rome, she's tall and he's short. How's he going to give her a kiss, or whisper something romantic in her ear? And so? So what. To solve the problem they'd have to go around with a ladder—there's no alternative.

I have to admit that Marilyn didn't have much to do with my obsession with blond hair. Poor Marilyn, they all used her and threw her away, including the Kennedy brothers. I wouldn't have expected it of J.F.K. What a disappointment! By the way, I've always wondered: did Jackie know about her husband's frequent betrayals or did she pretend it was nothing? I once read in a newspaper that Jack used to say, "If I don't go to bed with a woman every three days I get a migraine!" He said "woman," not "wife." Probably Jackie was very busy being the First Lady. Poor Jack, he didn't have any drugs available, he had to manage like a prehistoric male.

I was talking about my obsession with blond hair, right? The explanation should be sought in childhood, said Freud: perhaps the Barbie doll that my uncle Salem brought me from a trip to London bewitched me. For years I couldn't go to sleep without hugging her. This is a plausible hypothesis. The only certainty is that even as a small child I envied blond girls for their silky-smooth hair. My hair, on the other hand, was long, black, and curly, and I yelped in pain every morning before school when my mother combed it. As soon as I saw the comb, I ran away, like a hen that's about to have its neck wrung.

"Saaaafiaaa! Don't make me angry! Come here immeeeediately!"

"Mamma, you're hurting me."

"It's an order. Don't act like a spoiled child."

Me a spoiled child! No joking, please. It was my daily torture.

As time passed, my mania for hair didn't diminish but increased. So to the classic question that every child is asked, what do you want to be when you grow up, all my classmates would answer "doctor," or "architect." I, however, with great assurance and no hesitation, would say, "I want to be a hairdresser."

That's right: a hairdresser. I wasn't an idiot, I was a perfectly normal girl. I wasn't interested in provocation. But it was something very strong that I felt inside. One day my math teacher complained to my father:

"Your daughter doesn't apply herself enough in her studies."

"Why not?"

"Because she wants to be a hairdresser when she grows up."

"What? A hairdresser?"

"Yes, exactly. Just imagine! Hahaha."

All hell broke loose. My father got angry not only with me but also with my mother, holding her responsible for my lack of ambition. (The word "ambition" is a trap for women, as my grandmother will explain shortly.) Fortunately there was always Aunt Amina to come to my defense: "Dear brother, you're overdoing it with the child—it's not as if she wants to be a singer, or an actress, or a belly dancer, or something else immoral!"

This experience taught me how indispensable it is to keep your dream safe, and hide it, until the moment you can fulfill it. Talking too much is dangerous. I agree with the French when they say, "*Ceux qui parlent ne font pas et ceux qui font ne parlent pas*": those who speak don't act and those who act don't speak. So I decided to change strategies and convert to the collective dream.

"I want to be a doctor when I grow up, too. I'd like to cure children."

"How sweet. It's called a pediatrician. Bravo! Let's have a round of applause."

The most one can expect from a girl: a fledgling mother! All in order, nothing to worry about, the little girl is growing up in full obedience to tradition. A neighbor in Cairo, Uncle Attia, said, "Daughters are like hand grenades: it's best to get rid of them in a hurry!" If anyone asked how many children he had, he would always say, "Three boys, four hand grenades (to settle somewhere, inshallah), and two atomic bombs (one unmarried and one divorced)." Is it a coincidence that the word "bomb" in both Italian and Arabic is feminine?

The truth is that I understood early on, even before I read some books on feminism by Nawal Saadawi, that our society doesn't love women and above all doesn't tolerate ambition in them. My grandmother always urged us, her beloved granddaughters, "Don't get a swelled head, always fly close to the ground." And if someone ventures to fly high? The family will take care of breaking her wings. Ruthlessly.

First rule of survival: avoid competition with males in every way. In exchange for obedience a woman can enjoy male protection her whole life: from father to brother, from husband to son, from son to grandson. An Arab woman has to get one important thing through her head: to avoid complications she has to live like a sheep. What? Yes, like a sheep, and preferably white, not black. Better to be a normal sheep, conformist. If she abandons the flock she does it at her own risk and peril. She won't survive amid the herds of wolves! Clear?

In Egypt they say, "*Al maktùb aggabin, lazem tchufo l'ain!*" What's written on the forehead the eyes have to see. No one can escape *maktùb*, destiny. When we're born, God writes on the forehead of each of us what we will live until death. Someone will say: this is fatalism, the game is over, there's no free will, Muslims as usual, obedient to everything, blahblahblah.

It's not like that. *Maktùb* helps us accept what's already done, like the death of a loved person, in order not to fall into

deep despair, or go mad. There exists a higher will that domi-
nates ours. The matter is really rather complicated, but that's
natural, we're talking metaphysics, not physics.

The interpretation of my high-school Arabic teacher comes
to mind. Once in class there was a lively discussion about a line
from the Tunisian poet Abu al-Qasim al-Shabbi (poor man, he
was only twenty-five when he died). The line goes, "When the
people decide to live, destiny can but bend." Some of my classmates (probably budding fundamentalists) insisted that the
poet was an unbeliever and so he had better forget about paradise, the houri, the rivers of wine, and all the rest. In no case
can the will of the people surpass the divine will. God is above
the people. The professor explained that God is omnipotent
and can therefore change even destiny. It's a possibility to
reckon with, but it's up to us to pass the tests and show that
we're equal to it.

I've always liked this interpretation. To believe in *maktùb* is,
above all, an act of faith. Things don't happen by chance, there's
always a reason. What's important is to do one's best and accept
one's responsibilities. I like the concept of fair play in sports:
give a hundred percent and accept the final result. This in my
opinion is an example of *maktùb*.

ISSA

I spent a week considering the proposal, weighing the pros and cons. Spying is despicable work. You've got to meet a lot of requirements if you're going to be successful: don't look people in the face and have betrayal in your heart—as the Neapolitans say. But I'm no fool, I can't pretend not to notice: Islamic terrorists do exist, they're not an invention of the media. They've already shown the world what they're capable of; as a calling card the destruction of the Twin Towers was more than sufficient. So in the end I decided to accept.

I met with the SISMI captain again, again at the court in Palermo. He was pleased with my response. He gave me three days to get ready. It wasn't hard to invent an excuse to explain my absence: "I'm going to Tunis for work." My parents said nothing, they're used to their traveling son. But I had a hard time with Marta, my girlfriend. She wanted to know everything, as usual. She subjected me to her favorite quiz, the five "w"s: where, when, why, who, and what. Obviously she was disappointed by my answers—totally unsatisfied. But what could I tell her? I myself knew very little about the mission, and then, after all, I had to keep my mouth shut.

Judas and I arrived in Rome in the evening. We settled in an apartment in Via Nazionale. It was a real retreat. A ten-day intensive course. The absolutely first lesson was to use the English word "intelligence," rather than "espionage." Words are important, as Nanni Moretti said. I learned a lot of tricks by working on the character I was to play: a young Tunisian immigrant who is moving from Sicily to Rome in search of his fortune. In the meantime we moved to the familiar *tu* without much trouble.

"So, Tunisian, we have to find you an Arabic name. Do you have any suggestions?"

"I'd suggest Issa."

"Issa? What does that mean?"

"The equivalent of Jesus for Muslims."

"Jesus? The guy with the other cheek? We're starting well!"

"I like it."

"O.K., I understand. You want to be the good guy and I'm the bad guy, is that it? From now on call me Judas!"

Judas and Issa, a perfect couple. The devil and the holy water go arm in arm. During the retreat I read a stack of documents about terrorists. We looked at a lot of film clips. What struck me in particular was a documentary about Mohamed Atta, the head of the September 11th terrorists. His will is one obvious proof of his madness; for example he writes that he doesn't want pregnant women at his funeral. I saw a parade of terrorists, Algerian, Egyptian, Afghan, Pakistani, Iraqi, and others. All ready to sacrifice their youth to get to Paradise. Why in the world are they in such a hurry? Because the reward there is seventy virgins! Wow!

After a few days I had my residency permit, and so I could start my life as a non-European: I am Issa by name, Kamli by surname, Tunisian by birth and citizenship, unmarried. Luckily they didn't stick me with a wife and children. It's not a small point, because Marta is very jealous and, above all, impulsive. She would never give me time to explain to her calmly how things are: she acts impetuously, before I finished she'd hit me. She resolves everything in the end by begging my forgiveness with a wild outburst of tears.

During the preparatory phase of the mission I attended an important meeting. Little Cairo is a joint operation of the

SISMI, the C.I.A., and the Mukhabarat, the Egyptian secret service. Judas introduced two colleagues: an American named James and an Egyptian, Antar.

The meeting place was outside Rome, near Nettuno. The room was well equipped, the perfect setting for a spy thriller or a war movie. Photographs of the suspects in the first cell rolled by on a large screen. At the top of the list was Akram; there were the photos that showed him at Mecca.

Antar, my new Egyptian colleague, asked permission to speak and he made a couple of observations: "The dates on the photographs are extremely important; they're the incontrovertible proof that Akram did not go to Mecca for the ritual pilgrimage. On those particular days he should have been, like the rest of the pilgrims, in Medina, performing the various rites. The question is: what was he doing in Mecca?"

The American, James, answered quickly, "On the basis of reliable information we've discovered that Al Qaeda takes advantage of the period of the hajj to organize gatherings without attracting attention. It's impossible to check millions of pilgrims."

At the end of the meeting Captain Judas urged us all to be prudent: "Let's try not to make amateurish mistakes, as in the case of the three Egyptians in Anzio."

On the retreat, while we prepared for the operation, Judas had told me about that case. In October of 2002 three Egyptian immigrants in Anzio were arrested on charges of planning attacks on the American military cemetery in Nettuno, the McDonald's in Rome, and the Fiumicino airport. In their house the police had found a gun and about a kilo and a half of TNT. The press attributed great importance to a belt (immediately christened "the suicide-bomber belt") found in the closet of one of the three suspects eight days after the initial search. It turned out that it was the type of belt that the Muslim faithful wear when they go on a pilgrimage, to keep their money and documents safe. During the trial it emerged that the landlady had had a key role in the affair: in the preceding months she had quarreled frequently with the three suspects on matters having to do with payment of the rent. Further, it was discovered that she had had free access to the scene of the crime, thanks to the fact that the police had neglected to seal it . . . And what was the connection of the three accused men with Islamic terrorism? Only the testimony of a neighbor, an old man who stated that, while going up the stairs, he had heard one of them utter the name of bin Laden! In April, 2004, the Court of Assizes acquitted the three Egyptians of the charge of international terrorism, "because no crime was committed." In the meantime those poor wretches had done almost two years of prison. Who had wanted to set them up? And why?

SOFIA

There are scenes that stick in your mind like an unremovable tattoo. For example, I remember the day I cut my sister Nadia's hair for the first time. She was desperate, because she didn't have the money to go to a professional hairdresser. She couldn't miss her best friend's wedding, and she especially didn't want to make a bad impression on the other girls, who were all rich kids. She trusted me and I didn't fail her. I got it right on the first try. The haircut was stupendous and all her friends liked it.

So I became the underground hairdresser of the poor girls of the neighborhood. I didn't care about money, I accepted whatever they gave me. Often they gave me small presents: a shirt, a skirt, a purse, a fashion magazine. It was absolutely necessary to improve my technique, and, to keep up with the news of the profession, I devoured foreign women's magazines like *Femmes d'Aujourd'hui*, *Marie Claire*, *Elle*, *Vanity Fair*, *Vogue*, although tracking them down was a real undertaking.

As an adolescent one tends to think on a grand scale, without taking reality too much into account. My dream of becoming a hairdresser got bigger and bigger: a reference point of my existence, my reason for living. I dreamed of opening my own hair salon.

A dream is like a plant that grows day by day and produces good fruit as long as you don't neglect it. And I—I am very generous with my dreams. I give the best of myself. However, I did realize that the plan would be difficult to carry out in Egypt or any other Muslim country: with so many veiled women, where would I get my clients?

Little by little, I convinced myself that my dream would have to take place somewhere else: in Europe or America. Paris, London, Rome, Madrid, New York—why not?

I had no hesitation about choosing to study languages at the university. I threw myself into learning English and French. Luckily my knowledge of French helped me learn Italian when I ended up in Rome.

I graduated without any difficulty: I had the right motivation and the necessary enthusiasm. Many suitors knocked at our door to ask for my hand. Of course, I'm not a blonde, but still I'm a pretty dark-haired girl, typically Arab. I uttered many "No, thank you"s.

Among the candidates, however, a young man showed up who had emigrated to Italy but was from the neighborhood next to ours. His name was Said, he had a degree in architecture, and he said he was working as a chef in a big restaurant in Rome. An architect who works as a cook? It's the truth. Anyway, when I became his wife I discovered two things: first, that he wasn't a chef but simply a pizza maker. Second, that he's called Felice—"happy." In Egypt we say, "If your neighbor is happy, you become happy, too." I'm his wife, not his neighbor, and yet I still haven't seen all this happiness, at least not so far.

During our brief engagement my architect revealed that he had been in love with me since high school. How touching! He had loved me in secret. And yet I did not remember ever having seen him before.

I would say that he was rather lazy, what would it have taken to write me a love letter or send me a pretty red flower, remaining anonymous, of course. What a pity! Yet another secret love not returned.

As for the engagement, among us things are different: fiancés are permitted to hold hands, to sit in a café and have tea, exchange romantic words of love, but . . . but no sex before marriage. Kisses? Better not, or confined to the cheek. Let's be clear: to be engaged is one thing, to act like husband and wife is another. This I will not say again.

To simplify, we might say that engagement Egyptian style, Arab style, Muslim style is something like making a reservation, obviously after you've paid some money for the fiancée's *shebka*. This word refers to the jewels that are given to her, but it resembles *shabaka*, a word that means net, as in a fishing net. Now, the question is: who is the fisherman and who is the fish? What does the fiancé get in exchange? Well, he gets the right to publicly claim his future private property. Congratulations to the lucky beauty; finally, after years on display, she can leave the shop window. And, as the Italians say, "Good luck and may you have male children!"

After two meetings in the living room of our house I agreed to marry the architect. Was it a marriage of convenience, an arranged marriage? Of course. And what's wrong with that? Marriage can be arranged or not. There's no third way. The ones that aren't arranged have the same ending, anyway, with the refrain typical of all self-respecting soap operas.

Here's a taste:

"I thought you were generous, faithful, sensitive, affectionate, et cetera, et cetera. Instead, after the wedding . . . "

"Don't say that, I implore you."

"I thought you were the love of my life, the man with whom I'd raise children, travel, go shopping, grow old, and so forth. Instead, after the wedding . . . "

"That's enough, please."

"I thought you were my ideal. Instead, after the wedding . . . "

"Eeeeeenough!"

I have to admit that no one forced me to say the fateful "yes." Luckily, on questions of marriage my family tended to keep a low profile, so there was no pressure or, worse, blackmail of the type: "You should marry him without thinking twice, otherwise you'll find that you're an old maid with no future." Or: "Don't you see, my poor daughter, that your cousins (all of them) and friends (really all of them) are married, and that you're the only one who keeps looking?" In the case of advice I always say "Thank you." In the case of pity I'm ready with a "Go to hell" instead. Clear?

Basically I wasn't happy about the idea of the marriage itself, but I liked the idea of going to live in Italy: the Mecca of fashion. It was a sign of *maktùb*. I saw myself already managing a hairdressing salon or working with famous designers like Valentino, Versace, Armani, Gucci, Dolce & Gabbana . . . Why not?

I was sure that I would be successful in Italy. I had reflected a lot on the fact that women increasingly resort to cosmetic surgery. Apart from the high cost, there are serious health risks when the surgery fails. I've often seen on TV remade women who look like inflated monsters, with horrible breasts and clown lips. I said to myself—"These poor women, they don't know that the secret of feminine beauty lies in caring for their hair." Hair is half of beauty! Come on, wake up, ladies!

A few months ago I saw a show about the actress Michelle Pfeiffer on Channel 5. She was so beautiful in the film with Al Pacino where she played the waitress. But even she had had her lips touched up. In my opinion, she didn't need to. She should have gone to a good hairdresser rather than the operating room of a cosmetic surgeon. And let's talk about Melanie Griffith, who's married to Antonio Banderas: it seems that that poor woman is always sick because of drugs and alcohol. So what? So nothing. I prefer not to say anything else. You don't shoot at the Red Cross, or am I wrong?

My euphoria didn't last long. Unfortunately reality is stronger than dreams. A few days before the wedding the architect asked me to wear the veil.

"What did you say? I didn't hear you. Could you repeat that, please?"

"My love, you have to put on the veil."

"Is this a joke? Of course, and here I almost fell for it! You're a real Egyptian, what an actor. Hahaha."

"No, my love, I'm speaking seriously. This is a condition."

Put on the veil? Maybe I hadn't understood. Were we going to live in Italy or Iran? Is the veil compulsory in Rome? Felice was not joking at all. A real low blow. A blow below the belt. If we had been in the ring the referee would immediately have given him a warning and I would have gotten some points. Maybe I would even have won, in the end. Are there rules of the game to be followed, or am I wrong? The real problem is that we live in a society where the male is both the opponent and, at the same time, the referee. We women—what can we do? Will we ever win in this situation?

I tried very patiently to persuade him to give up his absurd condition, insisting on a fundamental point: the veil is not one of the five pillars of Islam and can in no way be used to measure a woman's conduct. Basically—let's be frank—the veil is just a bit of fabric. While faith is an infinite universe. In all intellectual honesty, I have to confess that that last sentence is not an arrow from my quiver. I don't remember where I heard it, but I like it a lot and every so often I pull it out. Good, eh?

I was like an impassioned lawyer, engaged to save an innocent child from the pyre: "I've done my five daily prayers ever since I was ten years old, I never forget to give the *zakat*, alms to the poor, I never skip a day of Ramadan, the only thing I haven't done to fulfill the obligations of Islam is the pilgrimage to Mecca (but I'm twenty-seven and there's still time, inshallah). In other words, I consider myself a good Muslim even without the veil." One couldn't be more clear and logical than that. Unfortunately, the architect wouldn't listen to reason; it was like talking to a stone. In the end I thought of breaking the engagement and cancelling the wedding, but the risks were too great. People wouldn't understand my motives.

"Hello, dear, I'm sorry the engagement was broken off. What can we do? It's *maktùb*. Tell me what happened."

"He asked me to wear the veil, a week before the wedding. Obviously I said no. That's the whole thing.

"You mean it's not because of your virginity?"

"Virginity? It has absolutely nothing to do with that."

"You mean the real reason is the veil?"

"Yes. That's the truth."

"The truth? You don't say! Hahaha."

If you think about it, in the Arab world breaking an engagement is like getting divorced without even getting married. What a joke! Thank God our society is an open book. Everything's clear. It doesn't take the genius of Einstein to get it. And I, luckily, am not a fool.

Anyway, I knew in advance that if the wedding didn't take place on the established day everyone would think that it was my fault, mine alone. I would never get away with it. The family of my former fiancé, seduced and abandoned, would have used a powerful weapon to discredit me and get their revenge: they would spread the rumor that the former fiancée (that is, me) wasn't a virgin. It's a trick that always works. And this would have ruined the reputation of my family and harmed the future of my sisters and my first and maybe even second and third cousins.

Instead of a hand grenade, I would become a new atomic bomb! And then I couldn't run that tremendous risk: to have on my conscience a dozen old maids!

Virginity, with us, is an obsession, something sacred. You don't play games with the bridegroom's trophy. In Morocco they say "*Ànnaq u bus wa khelli rahbat laàrùs*," "Hug and kiss, but don't touch what is reserved for the husband." So, diplomatically, I put off the problem of the veil until after the wedding. I thought that the question was still open. I was confident. Maybe a little too confident.

As for the veil: there are women who choose it freely, and their reasons can be various: out of conviction (they believe that the veil is the sixth pillar of Islam); for economic reasons (they save a lot of money on clothes); to avoid physical and verbal molestation in public places.

I waited a year and a half at my parents' house before I could get a visa for a family reunion. I arrived in Rome with my daughter on a summer day of suffocating heat. I was wearing the veil, just as my architect wanted. We came to live here, in Viale Marconi, where he had rented a small apartment: bedroom, small bedroom, living room, kitchen, and bathroom. We're on the fifth floor, but thank God there's an elevator. It's hard to climb all those stairs, especially on hot days, with the veil sticking to you!

In the early days it seemed to me that I was still living in Cairo. I saw so many Egyptians around that I wondered, a little astonished and bewildered, "Where is this Rome?"

ISSA

Am I getting to be a regular client of Little Cairo? It looks that way. I've been coming here for six days. Constancy is a virtue that never betrays you—sooner or later I'll be rewarded. It just takes a little patience and a lot of luck. Is there any danger of being found out? Don't be ridiculous. I'm a poor Tunisian immigrant who's come to Rome in search of a better future. New arrivals always need some reference point and I've found one in this place, among my Arab brothers. There's nothing odd about it.

I make the usual phone call to my "Tunisian mother." We've gotten to know each other better recently. She's rather a chatterbox, but that's good. Ten minutes is enough to find out the news: my "brother" Adel (older or younger?), who graduated four years ago, has found a job in a bank, thanks to the connections of "uncle" Ali. My "cousin" Mohsen has moved to France with his wife. Finally, my "sister" Amel is pregnant. This is really good news. I'll finally be an uncle. Shit!

After the call to Tunisia I decide to hang around at Little Cairo. I sit down next to two young guys (at a rough guess, I would say they're Egyptians) to watch Al Jazeera. There's a repeat of a program that's very popular in the Arab world. The format resembles a cockfight: there are two guests, experts with opposing opinions, and a moderator who plays the part of the impartial referee. The discussion today is heated, the subject is very much on people's minds: Is it right to export democracy to the Arab world by means of tanks, as happened in Iraq? Are the American neoconservatives right or wrong?

The adversaries are tough and the moderator conducts the game cleverly, he doesn't miss a chance to fan the flames. He always manages to set them against one another, for example: "What do you mean? The Arabs will never be able to achieve democracy by themselves? Then please explain to us, and without false nationalist rhetoric, what we should do." Or: "You declare openly that you are in favor of exporting democracy by force of arms. Then you're a traitor in the pay of the Americans. Respond to that charge from your questioner."

Arabs have a particular outlook, they see betrayal and plotting everywhere. It's a real disease that I've noticed in my travels in the Arab world.

I take advantage of a short ad to socialize with the guy sitting on my right. I, too, might have something to say on the subject, no? Anyone is allowed to make a comment on democracy. In other words, George W. Bush and his advisers don't have a monopoly on it. And so I move from words to action.

"Personally, I'm against the exportation of democracy as if it were merchandise."

"My friend, what does democracy have to do with it? The West just wants to colonize us again."

"You're right."

"Why aren't they taking democracy to North Korea or Castro's Cuba, eh?"

"It's true."

"They want our oil, that's the truth."

I go along with a nod of the head. Too bad, there's no time to continue the discussion, because the duel of the talking heads is starting up again. I have to wait for the next commercial. One of the two guests starts to raise his voice, or, actually, shout: "Westerners are hypocrites, they talk about democracy only when it's useful to them! For years they've supported the worst regimes in the Arab world." The other doesn't give in; instead, he starts raging like a wounded bull: "The only thing we Arabs are any good at is feeling sorry for ourselves and blaming the West for all our troubles. If we are oppressed, poor, unhappy, illiterate, sexually impotent and so forth, it's never our fault but that of the Western colonialists."

Suddenly I hear someone calling me. It's Akram.

"Tunisian!"

"Yes?"

"Are you still looking for a bed?"

"Yes."

"Then today is your lucky day! A place has become free in an apartment near here."

By now they all call me "Issa the Tunisian" or simply the Tunisian. I'm happy with that. Maybe I'll finally become a resident of Viale Marconi. Akram takes a piece of paper and writes the phone number of the landlady, a certain Teresa. He takes the opportunity to give me some useful advice. First of all I should call the lady immediately and tell her that I'm getting in touch with her on his recommendation. As a Sicilian, I know all too well the system of recommendations; everyone wants guarantees. Then I should insist on having an appointment today, there's the risk that the place will go to some other needy soul. Make your move before it's too late! Finally, he puts me on my guard against the greed of my future landlady.

"Teresa is a shit, she'll ask two hundred and fifty euros a month. She'll try to cheat you to take some trip at your expense."

"A trip at my expense?"

"Teresa has a nickname: Vacation. Get it?"

"No."

"She likes to travel, so she always needs money."

"So then how should I act with her?"

"Stick to two hundred euros. You have a residency permit, so she can't treat you like the tenants who don't have papers."

I nod without saying anything. I take Teresa's number and go into the booth to call her. Luckily, she answers after just three rings. She tells me to wait for her at Little Cairo because she's shopping at the supermarket on Via Oderisi da Gubbio. After this phone call I become aware of a problem I had completely underestimated: to seem credible I have to speak a labored Italian, even a little ungrammatical. Sometimes I forget the part I'm playing. I have to identify with the character of Issa, a Tunisian immigrant. I try to remember how my Arab acquaintances speak, especially the Tunisians. I even have to imitate their accent. The ideal is to speak an Italian with a dual cadence: Arab, because I'm Tunisian, and Sicilian, because I'm an immigrant who has lived in Sicily. Maybe the less Italian I speak the better. I promptly decide to temporarily suspend a lot of grammatical rules, so no more subjunctive or remote past. It annoys me to give up our beloved *passato remoto*.

After a few minutes Teresa arrives with two big shopping bags. She's around sixty, short, fat, round face, dyed red hair, and slightly overdone makeup. She has a relaxed face, I'd say slightly tanned—she seems to have recently returned from a vacation. In other words, the lady is in good health. They say that travel helps fight depression. The biggest problem of modern times consists in the refusal of the old to grow old. I read or heard this somewhere. But it's too intellectual for my taste. Intellectual nonsense. Today cheap travel to exotic countries is within reach of all pockets and all year round. Even cruises aren't exclusively for the rich anymore. Wow, how amazing—low-cost cruises!

Teresa alias Vacation tries to intimidate me linguistically with her Roman dialect. The problem is, though, that she has neither the fascination of Anna Magnani nor the charm of Alberto Sordi. Her voice is irritating; it reminds me of that politician who's on all the talk shows and news programs, and who seems like he's spitting when he speaks.

"Oh, goood, so you're also Egyptian?"

"No, I'm Tunisian."

"Afef's country!"

"Yes."

"Tunisia! Ahh, how nice. I been there four times, last year I went to Hammamet. I took the occasion to visit Craxi's grave. You know Bettino Craxi?"

I avoid telling her that in Tunisia Bettino Craxi is very well known.

And then I feel like showing off my Sicilian. Eye for an eye! But it's better not to, I can't afford to, under the circumstances. I've just got to lump it, the end. The man who holds his tongue lives a hundred years.

Anyway, it all went according to Akram's script. There were no surprises or dramas. We agreed on two hundred euros after a short but intense negotiation. Still, she did manage to trick me into an advance of three months. I've got to fork over the whole six hundred euros. So she can reserve a low-cost cruise at my expense? Don't be ridiculous. I'm not taking anything out of my own pocket. I'll be drawing on the funds of the Italian taxpayer. I'm on a mission for the good of my fellow-citizens. I'm now a very important employee of the State!

Business almost done, the bed is mine. I can move in tomorrow. Teresa asks if I want to see the apartment and I say yes. On her cell phone she calls one of the tenants, who works at the market nearby. After a while a short thin guy arrives. He's around thirty, his name is Omar, and he's from Bangladesh. His smile immediately strikes me. On principle I don't trust merchants and their broad fake smiles. It's a trick to get money out of you. That's how it always works.

Before I follow the Bangladeshi to the apartment, Teresa makes a date with me for tomorrow to finalize the agreement:

I'll have to give her the six hundred euros in cash. No checks or transfers. All under the table, naturally. I don't give a damn, since I'm on a mission.

On the way to see the house Omar gives me some advance information on my future fellow-tenants. He tells me, for example, that the majority are Egyptians. The minority is represented by a Senegalese, a Moroccan, and a Bangladeshi, that is, him. "The important thing is that we are all Muslims," he concludes, with a big laugh. The smile changes to a laugh? It's already better. Should I be worried?

The apartment is very close to Little Cairo; it's on the fourth floor. Omar takes me in, shows me the kitchen, the bathroom, and two bedrooms. There's no one home. I've got time to count the bunk beds. There are six. At first glance it seems like a dormitory.

After the tour I invite the Bangladeshi to the café for coffee. It's the least I can do to thank him for his trouble. We sit talking for quite a while. Actually, I say very little. The Bangladeshi tells me his story. He came to Rome ten years ago, after a long and expensive trip. His immigration was carefully planned. The family chose him because he was the best suited among his five brothers. Omar was lucky enough to go to school, so he can read and write, and also he was very healthy. Two important requirements for success as an immigrant.

Omar explains one important thing to me: every self-respecting immigrant has a plan for his immigration. Already, before he left, he had a strategy in place, with precise goals to be realized: building a house, marriage, acquiring land, contributing to the dowries of his sisters, paying for the schooling of his younger brothers . . . He's not just some poor devil who needs welfare.

Planned immigration is a kind of economic enterprise; it has nothing to do with the desperation of the illegal immigrants. In this case money, a lot of money, is invested in future earnings.

An immigrant like Omar becomes a small entrepreneur who is in the service of a family plan. He is willing to risk everything to become successful, for himself and his loved ones.

To get to Italy Omar relied on an organization that specializes in trafficking illegal immigrants, and he paid out a good ten thousand dollars. This sum was collected by the family, which went into debt up to its ears. From his native city in Bangladesh he left for Moscow with a tourist visa. Then he crossed many countries in Eastern Europe, to arrive illegally in Italy. Altogether the trip took two months.

At first he stayed with a cousin, in Brescia. Later he decided to join a childhood friend in Rome. Thanks to the last amnesty for immigrants, he became legal, so he could return to Bangladesh to visit his family, and he became engaged to a second cousin.

In these years of work and sacrifice, Omar not only succeeded in paying the debts contracted by his family for the journey but, through remittances, helped accomplish wonderful things: building a new house for his whole family, dowries for his sisters, etc. In other words, Omar is happy, because he did not betray the expectations placed in him.

At the moment my future fellow-tenant works at the market; he manages a vegetable stall with two other Bangladeshis. I don't understand why he accepts living in a dormitory rather than renting a single room, to have a minimum of privacy.

"My friend, the bed helps me save money."

"You manage to live with eleven people?"

"Of course. I've lived even with twenty people under the same roof!"

"How do you rest?"

"Rest? I'll rest, but not now and not here."

"When and where?"

"When I return to Bangladesh to get married."

To hell with privacy and repose! I'm still thinking like an

Italian, I can't put myself in the shoes of the non-European immigrant. Many of my fellow-citizens don't understand why the shops of the immigrants in Italian cities are open even on Sundays. But it's natural. They've come here to Italy to work, not to rest. In other words, they're not tourists! The adopted country becomes a sort of factory, where you work and pile up money.

Unfortunately we have to interrupt our interesting chat. Omar has to go back to work at the market.

I return to Little Cairo to thank Akram for his intercession. The cockfighting program on Al Jazeera is over. I sit down to watch the news. We're told about a chain of bombings in Baghdad. That's not news anymore. The story about the robbery of a tobacconist's shop or a pit-bull attack now makes a greater impression than the death of ten people in Iraq.

To distract myself from this succession of the dead and wounded I start making a little balance sheet of my mission. So far I've met a few people, mostly Egyptians. No one has yet invited me for tea or coffee, but I'm hopeful. I'm on a good path. The other day I met a Tunisian, a guy my age who works in construction. We had a nice chat between fellow-countrymen. At first I was disoriented, then I opened up. My "fellow-countryman" wasn't from Tunis, like me, but from Sousse, a little south of the capital. We talked about this and that, from the war in Iraq to the latest offers for prepaying your cell phone, from Italian politics to the Tunisian soccer championship. I pretend to be a fan of the Taraggi, a sort of Tunisian Juventus. Luckily I'm better informed about Tunisia than many real Tunisian immigrants. I always manage to amaze people, including myself.

I take the bus back to Via Nazionale. I send Judas a text message asking if I can see him right away. For reasons of security we can meet only in the usual apartment. I arrive in about twenty minutes. The captain is already there.

"News?"

"Yes. I found a bed in an apartment near Little Cairo."

"Wonderful! And good work, Tunisian. And?"

Judas doesn't like summaries; rather, he insists on details. He's a sort of professional gossip. In fact he wants to fully understand this business of the bed. Could it be a trap? A trick of Akram and his companions to check me out up close? Maybe they've already found me out? Bullshit. Still, the captain is right, we have to get rid of every doubt. Luckily, I have a solid, reliable memory, trained by the study of Arabic. The vocabulary of the Arabic language is really a good gym. You have to remember a lot of things. For example the word "sword" has a good three hundred synonyms. And so I tell him everything from A to Z. He keeps interrupting to ask for clarification or to make a comment. I listen to his instructions like a devout disciple before the venerable master.

"We're about to begin Phase 2 of the operation. Are you ready, Tunisian?"

"Yes."

"Now the game gets serious."

Judas is sure that the bed is a great opportunity. Now that I have a good cover, being a resident of the neighborhood, I can spend as much time as I want at Little Cairo, not just to call the "family" in Tunisia or watch Al Jazeera. Everything becomes easier: making new friends, spending time with the people there, and above all keeping an eye on Akram.

The fact of having this damn bed as a cover, however, creates greater expectations on the part of the captain. Now I'm going to have to work harder, and get concrete results.

Before dinner the most beautiful couple in the world arrives: Antar and James. The former is dark, the second fair, just like Starsky & Hutch. The C.I.A. agent is somewhat worried, because so far we haven't identified any suspect belonging to the second cell. At Langley, the C.I.A. headquarters, in Virginia, they want more information about Operation Little Cairo.

James tries to explain the point of view of his superiors: "Al Qaeda wants to show the world that the Americans are incapable of defending themselves, by attacking a symbolic and strategic place, like our Embassy in Rome." Judas tries to calm him, insisting on the fact that the Italian secret service patrols the neighborhood of Via Veneto day and night. Antar doesn't find this very convincing: "Al Qaeda tested its strategy when it attacked the American Embassies in Kenya and Tanzania. The bastards didn't miss a trick. They were really good. In my view it's not difficult to launch a rocket at a particular target or find someone willing to blow himself up in a crowd." James nods and confirms the analysis of his Egyptian colleague: "Attacking the American Embassy in Rome means humiliating not only the U.S.A. but also Italy, the European Union, and the Vatican. An attack like that would produce a tremendous wave of panic."

Judas listens in silence, then he gets up and goes out on the balcony to have a cigarette. At a certain point he turns to us, and says, in a serious voice, "We have to find the second cell, *immediately*."

Late that evening I pack a suitcase to take to my new home, and only then do I realize the significance of what Judas said about Phase 2 of the operation. I choose my clothes carefully, giving up my dark-blue suit, a couple of Pierre Cardin shirts, and three silk ties. It's not the right stuff for a non-European, unless he's a pimp, or a drug dealer. At the court in Palermo I saw all types. I also have to leave behind (briefly, I hope) all the objects connected to Christian Mazzari, like documents and photographs. I have the sensation of saying a final goodbye to this Christian who has been with me from birth. Before going to sleep I hear an inner voice saying, "You can't go back, and nothing will ever be as it was."

SOFIA

I call my family in Egypt once a week. I try to stay in touch in order not to succumb to the weight of homesickness. It's been two years since we went back. Why? We prefer not to go every year because of the cost. A round-trip ticket between Rome and Cairo is expensive. Then, there are gifts for the family members, of whom there are really a lot. Last time, we went into debt to pay all the expenses.

Every immigrant who goes home for vacation wants to demonstrate that he's been successful. In fact, he has to act like a rich guy, play the part of the American uncle. First of all, he has to dress like a movie star, then he has to hand out money right and left. The script is heavy and repetitious, and has to last the whole length of the visit. Worse than any soap opera. Mistakes are not tolerated. The performance has to be perfect.

My dear immigrant, I advise you strongly not to talk about the unpleasant or negative aspects of immigration. Like? Well, there's an embarrassment of choices. I'll be content to cite just a few examples: unemployment, off-the-books employment, high rent, racism, fear of losing your residency permit, absence of family etc. etc. But it's all pointless—no one will believe you. If someone asks, "How do you live in the West, in Europe, in Italy?" remember the right answer: "It's a paradise on earth!" This is fundamental. And there's no harm if you add a little something from your rich imagination.

Something like: when you arrive at the airport of Fiumicino for the first time you find anxious and desperate employers holding up signs: "Looking for workers. Food, lodging, and salary guaranteed." Not bad for a start, right? You're not obliged to accept an offer right away, since you just got there. You need to rest. Right? Work can wait.

On the train into the city you'll sit next to a beautiful blonde in a miniskirt and with the smile of a Marilyn Monroe. You'll chat about this and that, that is, simple things like politics and sports. When you reach the station, she won't let you go to a hotel, she'll insist on taking you home with her. I'm telling you, don't say no. Courage! You're very lucky. You won't sleep in the guest room but in her bed. Her bed? Yes, exactly. I won't tell you what you'll do all night, you can imagine it, no? And anyway, that's your business.

My friend, European women are not like the women of your country, they're not neurotic and backward, but open in every way. What did you say? I didn't hear you. Can you repeat that, please? You ask me about virginity? Hahaha. Don't worry, no one will force you to marry the blonde because you went to bed with her. That's no problem. Those things still happen in your country, but not here.

Let's keep going. Don't worry about documents, no one notices. Really? Of course! And the police checks? An urban legend. And the detention centers for illegal immigrants? They don't exist, like flying saucers and aliens. And the difficulties of learning the language? You can do without it. A pure formality: people communicate with gestures, like chimpanzees.

After a brief stay in the country called "Paradise on earth" you can go to the bank and ask for all the loans you want, at zero interest. You can buy anything: a Ferrari, a villa on Lake Garda, a new wife (docile as a sheep), and so on and so forth.

Don't wake the poor dreamers, don't break the spell, and above all never complain to those who stayed down there and can't wait to leave their hell for your paradise. And always remember: a person who has a toothache doesn't have the right to complain to a person who has cancer of the prostate or the brain. There's a limit to unseemliness. You have to feel pity for the people who've stayed down there, in the country of origin. In Italian "down" means low: when a person is sad or depressed, he says simply: I'm down. Get it?

You can understand, then, why many Egyptians delay the return home in the grand style—in order not to find themselves in this situation, which can be stressful and very upsetting. They say to themselves and their families, in a consolatory tone: "There's no *maktùb* for this year, may it be next year, inshallah!"

It's very tough to be truthful and tell things as they are. Immigrants prefer to lie to their relatives when they're unemployed, or exploited at work, or treated badly by the police, and so on. Why? They're afraid of not being understood, of being considered failures. That's the key word: failure. Every immigrant is condemned to be successful. Well? Well, nothing. He has to get rich. How? It doesn't matter how. In the end the result alone is what counts, or am I wrong?

I often go to the call center of my husband's friend. The place is frequented by Arabs, Egyptians for the most part. Akram, the owner, is very proud of the fact that he was one of the first immigrants ("No, really the first!" he maintains) to come and live in Viale Marconi. In some ways he can be compared to Christopher Columbus. Certainly he will be remembered in the history books of future generations as the pioneer of the Little Cairo of Rome. He places a high value on posterity, which explains the name he chose for his place: Little Cairo.

Akram is an important person in the life of our neighborhood. If he didn't exist, you'd have to invent him. He's an indispensable middleman for every type of business: renting a house, a room, or a bed, organizing a trip to Egypt or to Mecca, looking for a job or a wife, the renewal of a residency permit, application for Italian citizenship, and so on. To see him do his utmost for someone you would say he's altruistic and helpful, just like a volunteer from Caritas or the Red Cross. In reality his services aren't free. He's a shopkeeper to his marrow. Everything has its price. For example, if he helps you find a bed you mustn't try to be smart and think you can get by with a "Thank you" or a "God bless you." It's not done, it would be a serious discourtesy, Akram might be offended. It's better to give him some euros right away, to have him on your side. Someone like him can always be useful. He's a sort of master key.

He lives in Rome with his wife and three children. There are rumors, more and more persistent, about polygamy. There are even some who call him "the illegal polygamist" . . . But behind his back, not in front of him. It's said that he has two other wives, one in Egypt and one in Saudi Arabia. And that would explain his frequent trips abroad, in spite of the expense. Every year he goes to Mecca, "for the pilgrimage," he maintains. An excuse like that is full of holes! Islam says that a single pilgrimage in your life is more than enough to fulfill the fifth religious obligation. In other words, maybe he's substituted the pilgrimage for Ramadan, which has an annual rhythm. The question remains open: why does he go to Mecca every blessed year?

Akram knows all of our secrets. He's very skillful at getting people to talk. His questions are perfect traps, it's hard not to fall into them. He pays attention to the tiniest details and remembers everything. Some suspect that he has a system for intercepting all his clients' phone calls. It's not entirely impossible. It's not difficult to record calls; today there are sophisticated computer programs. And someone who possesses a mine of secrets can use them for manipulation or blackmail.

Akram is vain. For example he likes to be called *hagg*, pilgrim. It's a prestigious title, given to those who make the pilgrimage to Mecca or to an old person as a sign of deference. Today I'm in a good mood, I feel like making him happy.

Usually he calls me Madame; in Egypt that's a respectful way of addressing a woman. It's one of the French words that have remained in Egyptian speech.

"Hello, *hagg* Akram."

"Hello, Madame. How are you?"

"Fine."

"Health?"

"Thank God."

"Work?"

Work? Akram coming out into the open! This is not a mistake, it's a message. He's asking about work, though he knows that, at least officially, I'm a housewife. What is he alluding to? Well, at this point, it's likely that he knows—that for a year I've been secretly working as a hairdresser at my friend Samira's house. I have a couple of clients every week. My husband is in the dark about the whole thing.

For now Akram prefers to keep his mouth shut. What will he want in exchange for his silence? Sooner or later I'll find out. I try to smile, to hide my embarrassment. I go into an empty booth and call my sister Zeineb, but no one answers. I dial the number of our house in Cairo.

"Hello, mamma."

"Hello, my dear. How are you? And how is your husband and the little one?"

"We're all fine, mamma."

"So you'll come next summer?"

I expected this question. I have an answer ready: "There's no *maktùb* this time, maybe next year, inshallah." I avoid telling her the truth, which is that we can't afford the cost of the trip and all the rest. It's so frustrating! I miss them so much. I feel like crying, but I try to hold back my tears. Luckily I manage to pull myself together, thanks to two nice surprises that my mother has for me. First, this year my parents will make the pilgrimage to Mecca. I'm happy for them. My father was very set on it. Second, my younger sister, Layla, is getting married at the end of the year, after five years of engagement. She and her fiancé finally found a house.

When I hang up I realize that tears are falling down my cheeks. I open my purse and look for a tissue, but I can't find one. Damn! I don't want Akram to see me in this state, but I can't stay shut up inside here all day. As I'm coming out of the booth a young man with a mustache offers me a tissue. I take it and thank him. He doesn't say anything, but he smiles at me. I've never seen him before. I dry the tears and go to Akram to pay.

On the way home, I easily identify the reason for my tears: the fact that I won't be present at my sister's wedding really makes me sad. It's hard not to share important moments like this with your family.

To deflect the sadness I start philosophizing about marriage and divorce. For an Egyptian Muslim girl like my sister Layla, getting married will not be the end of her journey but, rather, the start. The tests never stop. You have to get ready for other challenges, of which the absolutely most important is: never get divorced! The divorced woman carries the burden of failure her whole life. She is condemned to death and executed countless times. Every look is an accusation, every judgment a death sentence. What? Death sentence? Yes, it really is. Social death is crueler than physical death. Where can a woman without a husband, and without her virginity, go? Nowhere. If she's widowed the situation is different, because it's not her fault. It's a question of *maktùb*. In the case of divorce, on the other hand, you don't disturb Signor *Maktùb*. There's no use looking for a scapegoat. The divorced woman is the only offender. The perfect offender.

It's hard to explain to people here that for us when a woman marries she changes guardians: she moves from her father's jurisdiction to her husband's. It's like a shop that changes owners. At first there is plenty of hope and, especially, enthusiasm. But after a while you realize that the situation hasn't changed; in fact, in certain ways it's worse. "We were better off when we were worse off," as Grandfather Giovanni says. (I'll have occasion to talk about him later, he's very entertaining.)

Anyway, the important thing is for the bride to emerge safe and sound from the market of unmarried women. It's not a small thing. The market of divorced women, on the other hand, is utterly the worst, full of predators, profiteers, and every sort of gawker. It's better to be an old maid than divorced. I have no doubts about that.

The wedding is only the first test, I was saying. I, for example, thank God, passed the test of virginity with no problems, after a very embarrassing night. We were both virgins, even though with us it seems that virginity is a feminine monopoly. Men who have never done it are simply "inexperienced." My husband is a practicing believer, before me he had never gone to bed with a woman. This is quite an advantage. I'm sure he won't betray me. Not because he loves me, but out of fear of God. Conjugal faithfulness is assured. You Italian women, don't go saying "Lucky you." It's no bed of roses. Marrying a fervent Muslim has advantages and disadvantages. My friend, if you marry a man like that you have to expect some inconveniences; for example, polygamy. Oh yes. It's part of the package, take it or leave it. Let's see how you manage to compete not with one but with three women! You want a scene from a soap opera that introduces the subject of polygamy?

"I've decided to take another wife, dear."

"Why?"

"Because I have the right to have four wives. Don't tell me you've forgotten."

"What have I done to deserve such a punishment?"

"*C'est la vie, ma chère.* I'm a man and I can do as I like."

"It's not right."

"That's what you say, my dear! Hahaha. I follow the teachings of the Koran."

"The Koran isn't very clear about polygamy."

"That's what you say, my dear! Hahaha. I'm only following the example of the Prophet."

Polygamy in Islam: what confusion. And so? So what. I should explain. I would agree that the Koran is the word of God, but it always requires an interpretation. Here is the root of the problem: a woman's interpretation of the Koran still doesn't exist. Not one. It's a male monopoly. Women are excluded from so many things. For example, there's no verse, or *hadith*, that prohibits a woman from being an imam. In spite of that, I've never once in my life seen a woman leading prayers.

The truth is, Muslims who are continually citing the Prophet Mohammed, and then, safe at home, beat their wife and children, make me angry. Our Prophet was not a violent man. I know his story, I find it absolutely ridiculous to reduce his great example to polygamy. Even if he lived fourteen centuries ago, I think he's very advanced compared to the Muslims of today.

Would you like to talk about polygamy in the Koran? I'm not afraid. I'm ready. I didn't study at the religious university of Al Azhar, but I've read a ton of books on the subject. So: there are just three lines on the subject of polygamy and they are found in the chapter titled "Women." Here's exactly what they say: "Among the women you like, marry two or three or four, and if you're afraid you can't be fair to them, then one alone." End of quotation. In my humble opinion, polygamy is linked to conditions that are impossible to fulfill. I would like to see how Signor Polygamist will be fair to four wives! In fact, he'll have to divide everything precisely into four: time, money, kisses, presents, and so on. It's easier to see the moon at midday than to treat four women in the identical way. It's a real mess, and leads straight to the insane asylum. Poor polyga-mist? Poor my foot! His bad luck.

Yet, and I'm sorry to say this, the battle against polygamy was lost from the start. Why? I've already explained it. O.K., let's repeat it for the last time: in Muslim society the male is the opponent and the referee at the same time. Is it clear now?

Anyway, I personally don't have to worry too much, because my husband isn't rich. Polygamy is a luxury, and not all Muslims (I would add: luckily) can afford it.

My wedding night? I would say that it went well, in spite of our lack of experience. I don't feel like recounting the details. I'm a little embarrassed. And then Islam prohibits spouses from speaking to third parties about their sex life. What happens in the bedroom should remain top secret. But everyone knows that we women talk too much. We often let ourselves go with our best friends, who in turn have other best friends, and so on. In the end marital secrets lose their value and become the subject of gossip. I, however, am careful about these things.

The test of virginity is only the first on the list. Right afterward comes the test of fertility. Because in Muslim society sterility is cause for divorce. If the couple doesn't succeed in having children it's always the woman's fault, as if impotence and male sterility didn't even exist.

Thank God I got pregnant right away. Another important test passed. Great joy all around. And right away the expectations started: let's hope it's a male! The name had been ready ever since my father-in-law died, may God have mercy on his soul. Instead, Aida arrived. She's four now, and she's the light of my life. She was born in Cairo, nine months after the wedding. I didn't waste any time. How good I've been!

Thank God traditions, especially the ones that are harmful to women, don't last for eternity. Everything comes to an end, and God Almighty remains. Because, sooner or later, change arrives, like the sun when it melts mountains of ice. In my grandmother's time, a woman who gave birth only to girls was considered half sterile, and seriously risked being divorced. Fertility is bound up with the procreation of males. All the husbands of that time were very demanding; they were considered kings and they wanted a male heir. A man who has only daughters is only half a father, and for that he deserves compassion: poor man, he's *Abu al-banat*, a father of girls!

The early days in Italy were really hard. When I went out on the street, people looked at me morbidly, almost obsessively. I wondered: Was I walking around naked? And then in their eyes I often saw irritation, uneasiness, impatience, and fear. And I wondered: Why are they afraid of me?

After a while I discovered the answer: my veil was like a traffic signal where people had to stop. That obligatory stop was the ideal moment to unload tensions, fears, worries, anxiety, et cetera. People needed to vent. I was like the punching bag that fighters use for training. In fact, when I walked in the neighborhood of Viale Marconi I was never alone. I was always arm in arm with a crowd of ghost companions: their names? Jihad, holy war, suicide bomber, September 11th, terrorism, attacks, Iraq, Afghanistan, Twin Towers, bombs, March 11th, Al Qaeda, Taliban. And so on. In other words, I was a sort of bin Laden disguised as a woman. People must have been afraid, of course. So little by little I figured out a way. I had to resist in order not to isolate myself within the four walls of my house, a path that leads directly to depression.

I decided to intervene. First of all, I threw myself into studying Italian. Then I began to wear colorful veils. I eliminated black, because it symbolizes mourning and grief. I like to combine colors: a pink, green, or purple scarf with a white, blue, or gray outfit. I try always to be smiling. Our Prophet says: "A smile is like giving alms." I struggled not to lose faith in myself. But what a lot of work!

I have to say that the situation has improved now. At first

the veil obsessed me, day and night, it was a fixed idea. I was afraid it would be a real obstacle to fulfilling my dream. No one would dare go to a hairdresser with a veil. And so? So what. I kept having the same nightmare: Marilyn wearing a veil, and in tears! The only way to get rid of it was to convince my husband. I used every trick, I even told him that the son of an Egyptian in a veil who lived on Viale Marconi refused to go to school because his classmates made fun of him: "Your mamma is a Taliban!" "You're the son of a Taliban," or "Your mother is bin Laden's sister." Removing my veil would be good for our daughter. Why have her grow up with complexes?

Unfortunately, my husband didn't want to hear about it, and he just kept repeating the same phrase: "The wives of all my friends wear a veil—what will the Egyptians and the other Muslims of Viale Marconi say about me?" Damn, all he thinks of is himself, his own reputation. He doesn't care a dried fig about me. He's not the one with the veil.

ISSA

A week has passed since I moved to this apartment. I've had tremendous problems adjusting; I can't sleep at night more than two hours in a row. What should I do? It's not my fault if I've always had a room to myself. For the same reason, I've acquired certain habits, like sleeping nude, temperature permitting, or reading before I go to sleep; I love biographies of famous people. Here it's not a good idea to be the self-taught intellectual immigrant and passionate reader. In other words, I've been forced to quickly change my habits, and I immediately renounced my nighttime nakedness. I might be taken for a pervert or a gay, more than sufficient reason to be thrown out of this apartment. Muslims are real male chauvinists, openly homophobic. While we Italians, sly as usual, are friendly toward gays and women but underneath we're—hypocritically—chauvinist.

I still can't understand how people manage to sleep with the light on. There's always someone who comes home from work after midnight or goes out at dawn. Not to mention the roar of faucets, of chairs being dragged . . . The result is that I'm suffering from insomnia, a problem I've never had before. I've always slept easily, even when I'm traveling and constantly sleeping in a different place. The discomfort is obvious, it's not just a whim of mine. I'm not just playing the spoiled child, used to luxury. This is a serious problem. If I don't sleep well I'll have some trouble concentrating on my mission, won't I?

Don't complain, little one, as my grandfather Leonardo used

to say, may his soul rest in peace. Let's look at the glass half full. One of the positive things about this complicated week is that I'm gradually starting to know all eleven of my fellow-tenants: eight Egyptians, a Moroccan, a Bangladeshi, and a Senegalese. I'm also busy getting familiar with the space. For example, I've noticed that the kitchen is transformed, in emergencies, into a makeshift dormitory to welcome a couple of guests—relatives, friends, or friends of friends of one of the tenants.

Everyone knows that Arabs are very hospitable. For centuries they've cultivated this grand passion, helped by the vastness of the Sahara, by its immense spaces. What does it take to put up a tent and spread a carpet for guests? Nothing. What does it take to feed them? A cup of milk and some dates. Unfortunately, we don't live in the desert, amid camels and palm trees. Hospitality has become expensive and has lost its deep value. In Italy you're not allowed to put up someone at your house without declaring or reporting (what a terrible word) him to the local police station within forty-eight hours. This is a law that goes back to the seventies; its purpose was to combat terrorism. Hospitality no longer has to do exclusively with the private life of individual citizens; the State insists on knowing who sleeps at your house. Let's be frank: for us Italians the existence of a law is one thing, its application another. The usual split between theory and practice, fed by our allergy to legality. In other words, in terms of public safety I and my eleven fellow-tenants are illegal residents; none of us have the proper requirements to live on Viale Marconi.

I've noticed that in our building there are a lot of students (mostly girls), owing to the proximity of Roma Tre University. The other day I met a student at the entrance of the building, she had come for an interview about renting a place to sleep. An interview for a job? No, an interview for a bed. Just that. It seems like a mistake, but it's not. She had tears in her eyes, because it hadn't gone well.

I stopped to listen to her; she really needed someone to talk to, right away. I did my best to hide my Italianness and play the role of the Tunisian immigrant. The girl had no prejudices: venting to a non-European was fine with her. Where had the problem originated? The landlord was looking for a student who would also do the housecleaning. Insane. There was something that didn't make sense: was the poor girl supposed to study and graduate or was she supposed to be the domestic help? This shit went off his rocker, maybe the next time he'll want a student who's a belly dancer or a sushi chef or just gives blow jobs. All this for a damn wretched place to sleep.

The girl asked me to help her look. I thought of giving her my place, but I immediately abandoned that idea. It can't be done. An Italian girl together with five young men (of Muslim religion, a not negligible fact) in one room? I already see the newspaper headlines, unleashed like pit bulls: VIALE MARCONI. FIVE NON EU MUSLIMS RAPE ITALIAN STUDENT. No, that's no good, it's too long. You need something short but striking, like: MUSLIMS RAPE STUDENT. There, that would be the perfect headline, extremely suggestive and with many possible interpretations. For example, the word "Muslims" could be understood as "all Muslims," that is, a billion and a half people! The result, in the mind of someone who's already slightly prejudiced: throughout the world there are a billion and a half rapists who belong, without exception, to the same religion!

Those poor students who come from outside Rome, taken advantage of by unscrupulous landlords. I should be compassionate toward them, because they have to put up with the same problem of lodgings as immigrants. In fact, maybe they're in a worse position, because it's really terrible to feel like a foreigner in your own country.

Our apartment is no bigger than sixty square meters: kitchen, bathroom, and two bedrooms. There is constant activity, twenty-four hours a day—it's like being in an emergency room. There are at least four of us who work at night, in restaurants.

Sixty square meters! If you divided this space by twelve we'd have five square meters a person. This is the sort of calculation that's usually made by lawyers on behalf of their jailed clients, to rouse the pity of judges and obtain a reduction in jail time, or to solicit the compassion of members of parliament and urge them to pass a law on pardons. But does this mean my room is a cell? Don't be ridiculous.

And yet the comparison between Teresa's apartment and jail isn't completely absurd. Besides the problem of overcrowding, there is a code of honor that has to be respected. My experience as an interpreter at the court in Palermo has brought me into close contact with the world of prisons, and I can decipher certain behavior easily. The code of honor is based on hierarchy and unwritten rules. Anyone who doesn't understand or pretends not to understand runs the risk of being punished. The worst punishment is not violence but exclusion from the group. That is exactly what I would like to avoid at all costs. I want to be accepted and liked by everyone. So I stick to the code of honor unconditionally.

Let's see what I've learned. First, there is a hierarchy based on religion, even if we're all Muslims. The observant have a privileged status; for example, they have precedence in the use of the kitchen and, especially, the one bathroom. The reason? The ablutions for performing the five daily prayers must be done at precise times. The *salat*, the prayer, is a sort of appointment with God, and it's very important to arrive punctually, a mark of respect. So the line for the toilet is only for the non-observant like me. And if you wet your pants? That's your problem! You have to cope by dashing out to some café on Viale Marconi. Luckily you can find one every two feet.

Further, you're strictly forbidden to bring alcohol, pork,

or—above all—women into the house. Except for the tiny photograph of Simona Barberini in the room where I sleep (obviously not taken from the famous calendar in which Simona appears without veils), there's not a trace of a woman in this lousy apartment.

Smokers are tolerated provided they smoke outside, on the little balcony off the kitchen. And if it's cold and raining or snowing? It's their problem. Anyway, they should thank God that the fatwa declared by the Taliban against cigarettes hasn't yet found adherents among the tenants. But you never know. The future, as they say, is unpredictable.

Then, there is another hierarchy, of a different nature, based on native country: the eight Egyptians feel that they are the true landlords. Maybe they've been infected by that shitty virus that strikes all majorities, always and everywhere: screw the minorities!

All the food cooked here is based on Egyptian cuisine. The paintings hanging in the kitchen and in the two rooms are reproductions of the Pyramids or some tourist village in Sharm. Above the refrigerator waves a small Egyptian flag. Clearer than that . . .

It goes without saying that Egyptian Arabic is the official language within the walls of the apartment. The music is Om Kalthoum (she's the Egyptian Maria Callas). I don't like her because she always repeats the same passage over and over. Arabs are mad for repetition—is that why they accept being governed for life by the same people?

In other words, we live in a sort of Egyptian enclave in Italian territory. The non-Egyptian tenants are divided into two categories. Mohammed, the Moroccan, and I are in second place; we're Arabs and we can communicate linguistically with the majority, limiting insult and injury where possible. But for the Senegalese and the Bangladeshi there's no escape: they're at the bottom. They have to submit or leave. To be

Muslim isn't enough. It's better to be an Arab Muslim, but it would be fantastic to be an Egyptian Arab Muslim!

Finally, we have a third hierarchy, this one imposed from the outside. We live not on an autonomous island but, rather, in a society that conditions our choices and limits our freedom. So we are divided into illegals, on one side, and legals, on the other.

The former live in panic; they are terrified by the idea of being arrested, shut up in some camp, and expelled. They talk obsessively about an amnesty that would enable them to obtain a residency permit. They wish to be out in the open—they don't want to hide as if they were criminals. They are always afraid of the police and especially the carabinieri. They're constantly being blackmailed.

"Now I'm calling the police!"

"Please, don't ruin me."

"So you're afraid of the police? And if I call the carabinieri, you'll piss in your pants?"

"Please don't, I implore you, on my knees."

The legal immigrants, on the other hand, can take advantage of a discount of fifty euros on the rent (this was established by the finance company Teresa alias Vacation). An even greater advantage is that they don't have to tremble with fear when they hear words like police, carabinieri, expulsion, detention center, Northern League, and so on.

"Now I'm calling the police."

"I'll give you the number, you piece of shit."

"I see, you're not afraid of the police. Then I'll call the carabinieri!"

"What are you waiting for, asshole?"

I share a room with four Egyptians and the Senegalese. I immediately hit it off with the Egyptian Saber, who sleeps in the bed under mine. I like him a lot; he's very entertaining. He was born in Cairo twenty-three years ago. He's the typical boy next door: fashionable clothes, hair styled with gobs of gel, latest-model cell phone. Physically, he looks like an Italian, let's say a southerner, a handsome, dark Mediterranean—like me! He could pass for a purebred Italian if he kept quiet, but that would be impossible, because Saber is an incurable chatterbox. His problem is that he can't pronounce the letter "p," and to survive linguistically he clings, like a desperate shipwrecked sailor, to the "b." When he says the word "brostitute" people think he's Sicilian, otherwise it's kind of a mess. He's lived in Rome for four years, but he doesn't have a residency permit. He works as an assistant pizza maker, hoping he'll soon be promoted to pizza maker and earn a little more.

Saber has asked me to talk to him in Italian. "Because I communicate in Arabic, and work and live with Arabs, I forget I'm in Italy!" he says, laughing. He is constantly talking about girls and soccer. His great dream is to become a famous soccer player. Next to the bed, on the left, is a poster of Paolo Maldini. Saber is a fan of Milan. I, like many Sicilians, root for Juve. Luckily I don't have to hide this passion. I'm not in the least worried: there are plenty of Juventus fans among the immigrants.

Soccer is not Saber's only passion. The other is called Simona Barberini. Next to the bed he has a small photograph of her cut out of a magazine. Before he goes to sleep he gives her a good-night kiss, and when he wakes he opens his eyes to her smiling face.

"You see how beautiful Simona is? Someday she'll be mine."

"Be careful, too much dreaming can be dangerous."

"Issa, all I need is a minute to win her over. You've never seen me at work. When I enter the field there's no room for the competition."

"How will you get to her?"

"No broblem. She'll come to me."

Saber explains his theory, letting me in on a few things I didn't know about Simona Barberini. This beautiful Italian girl falls in love easily with rich and famous athletes. Also, she had a love affair with an Arab emir a few years ago. So she wouldn't have any prejudices against Arabs and Muslims. Truthfully, there has to be a difference (a great big difference) between an emir and an illegal Egyptian immigrant. But Saber doesn't bother much with this detail, because he has worked out a plan that anticipates four phases. First: become a legal immigrant. Second: break in as a soccer player, preferably for Milan, but the important thing is to play in Series A. Third: get on TV a lot, in order to attract attention, ideally as a regular guest on some famous soccer talk show. The ultimate would be to get a part in a comedy with Christian De Sica. Fourth: win the heart of Simona Barberini.

A perfect plan, no denying it, except for one small observation: wouldn't it be useful to devote some attention to the pronunciation of Italian? Is there no hope of recovering that damn "p"? But I prefer not to be critical—I don't want to ruin the magic.

Our room resembles a warehouse. And this is because of Ibrahima, the Senegalese. His big bags of counterfeit goods are scattered here and there, under the beds and on top of the closet. If the police turned up, we'd all end up at the precinct.

Ibrahima has been in Italy for fifteen years; he lived in the north for a long time, before settling in the Eternal City. He has no sympathy for the Lombards, but he can't rid his speech of their slang and their locutions. He's thirty but looks older. He belongs to that category of young men who seem in a hurry to get old. Young men let themselves go physically when they lose interest in courting the opposite sex, as happens frequently to those who are married. This I read in some magazine—another piece of intellectual bullshit!

He has five children, who are with his wife, in Dakar. He was married when he was still a teenager; in Africa marrying early has a long tradition. Proudly, he shows me a photograph of his oldest son, who's now in high school and in a couple of years will go to the university. Ibrahima's dream is for him to be a doctor. But dreams are never free, you have to pay to fulfill them. He supports his family, thanks to the remittances he sends—two hundred euros every month. He's a peddler of counterfeit goods, like the majority of his countrymen, running a thousand risks every day. He hates the local police and the customs police. Luckily he doesn't know that my father, my real father, is a cop in Mazara del Vallo.

"Brother, the cops are pieces of shit. They break your balls every day. They treat us worse than thieves."

"Selling counterfeit goods is illegal."

"So, what the hell! We buy and sell, where's the harm? It's called commerce."

"But it's against the law."

"Brother, the market and the sidewalks belong to the people."

"No, you're wrong. They belong to the city."

"Come off it!"

I immediately regret having acted the moralist. I could have spared him these fucking lessons on legality. The law is always on the side of the strong and the rich. I mustn't forget I'm from Sicily. There's quite a difference between those who can afford to pay an experienced lawyer and those who have to make do with some greenhorn chit. Like hell are we all equal before the law!

I have to admit that I've always admired the foreign street peddlers like Ibrahima. They are true anarchists, revolutionaries in the field of commerce. They don't give a damn about licenses or taxes; they do everything openly. The market should be open to all, it's a place of meeting and exchange. I don't understand why the city governments give the peddlers such a hard time. I recall the Francesco Rosi film *I Magliari*, with Renato Salvatori and the great Alberto Sordi. The story is set in Germany in the fifties and recounts the adventures of a group of illegal, crooked fabric merchants, in other words, Italian street peddlers.

The third tenant I've socialized with in the past few days is the Moroccan, Mohammed. He's forty-five and has been in Italy since 1988; until two years ago he lived in Rome with his wife and two children. They were evicted, so he decided to send the family home to Morocco, and he rented a bed. Mohammed feels this situation as an injustice; he doesn't think he deserves it, since he has always been an honest worker. He's also slightly depressed because he hasn't received his new residency permit. He's a carpenter, a dangerous job that requires intense concentration.

"Some day or other I'll cut the fingers on one hand and they'll throw me out of work without a second thought. My head isn't right."

"You have to pay attention."

"I can't. I went to the doctor and he gave me some tranquilizers and sleeping pills."

"It's a bad time, but it will pass."

"I even got an ulcer. I've been waiting for the new residency permit for a year and a half."

Mohammed tells me about his odyssey for the residency permit—a long, ugly story. The latest immigration law reduced the term of the permit from four years to two, and the police stations, which handle the permits, freaked out. The renewal shouldn't take more than three weeks. But that's a purely theoretical time frame. In practice, immigrants have to wait Biblical lengths of time, as long as two years, so it's possible to get a residency permit that has already expired. While you're waiting for a new document you're issued a small coupon, just a piece of paper with a number on it, which has no legal value: the holder can't open a bank account, travel abroad, buy a car, legally rent a house, and so on. It's not even any good for wiping your ass! In effect, the immigrant becomes semi-illegal, held hostage by the law.

My fellow-tenant has a full heart and wants to relieve himself. He talks about the racism he's had to endure in Italy.

"The word 'Moroccan' doesn't refer to someone from Morocco. It's an insult, that's all, like nigger, fag, bastard . . . You know why the Italians hate the Moroccans so much?"

"No, why?"

"They say that during the Second World War Moroccan soldiers raped a lot of Italian women."

"But that really did happen."

"I don't deny it. But why should I pay the price? And then those soldier bastards fought under the French flag, not the Moroccan. Shouldn't they have been arrested and punished for what they did?"

Mohammed's words make me reflect on the imaginary Italian collective. The women raped by Moroccan soldiers during the Allied advance toward Rome were called the "Marocchinate." The whole episode is still taboo, in spite of *La Ciociara*, the great De Sica film. Italian soldiers, too, were guilty of rape, in Ethiopia and Somalia. *U lupu r'a mala cuscienza comu opera piensa*—the wolf with a bad conscience thinks the worst of everyone. Is it right to blame the poor Moroccan immigrants of today?

After lunch I stop off at Little Cairo. I glance quickly at the news on Al Jazeera, there's a story on the war in Iraq. Unfortunately the situation gets worse every day. By now people are speaking openly of civil war, total war, between Shiites and Sunnis, between Kurds and Arabs, between Muslims and Christians. In short, all against all. There are plenty of Iraqis today who look back nostalgically at Saddam Hussein. They say that at least during the dictatorship you didn't die in a bombing while you were shopping at the market or attending a funeral. You can see they've forgotten the repression, the torture, the assassinations, and the slaughters suffered during the time of Saddam.

Later I decide to call "my family" in Tunis. I dial the number, the "mamma" doesn't answer, as usual, but a male voice. "Hi! It's your brother Adel. How are you?" I don't remember if he's older or younger than me. But it's a marginal fact. The important thing is to keep up the conversation by asking circumstantial questions. How are you? What are you doing? How's the family? Friends? Neighbors? I'm content just to listen to his answers. My "brother" focuses on his new job at the bank and I let him talk. Every so often I stick in some nonsense to maintain appearances and encourage him to go on.

At a certain point I turn to my right and I see a girl in a veil who is weeping as she talks on the phone. Shit, what a beautiful girl! Her expression gets to me. I look at her for a few minutes while I'm pretending to listen to Adel. She's so overwhelmed that she's not even aware of her tears. Suddenly she returns to reality, tries to arrange her scarf, digs in her purse but doesn't find what she's looking for. I can see what she needs. I say goodbye to my "brother" and hang up. I leave the booth, and wait for the girl to finish her call and come out.

"Here, take this tissue."

"Thank you."

I can't see her face too well. But the word "thank you" is enough for me to guess that she's Egyptian and to register the sound of her voice. I watch her go to Akram to pay; she leaves without turning around. I'd like to know who she is and why she was crying. I'm tempted to follow her, or at least ask Akram for information. He knows everyone and could surely satisfy my curiosity, but I resist. A veiled young woman on Viale Marconi can't be a student, so very likely she's a married woman. Better not to take the risk. I have to control myself in order not to compromise the mission.

Around six I go to my appointment with Captain Judas in Via Nazionale. I arrive early and take the opportunity to have a shower. I'm disgusting, smelly, I stink like a fish seller or a tramp. In the Viale Marconi apartment if you want to wash you have to get up at dawn, before the others, because the hot water heater barely functions. The hot water is gone after one shower, at most two. The landlady acts like a deaf-mute, she has no intention of coughing up the money to buy a new one. She's hoarding for another vacation. So you have to settle for whatever works. Many of us heat water in the kitchen for an old-fashioned shower, with a big cup and basin.

After the shower, while I'm waiting for Judas, I go online to check my e-mail. There are fifty e-mails in the in-box: three from my (real) sister, Elena, two from my (real) brother, Carlo, one from my (real) little sister Sandra, and fifteen from Marta. What happened? I read the messages from my girlfriend in chronological order backwards. Luckily nothing to worry about. Of course, she wants to know how I am and especially why I haven't been in touch. She's right—she's not being unreasonable or capricious. I should call her right away. As a precaution I use a prepaid phone card. Officially I'm abroad.

"Hi Marta, it's Christian."

"Love! How are things in Tunis?"

"Fine, you?"

"Why haven't you called? Why haven't you answered my e-mails? Why . . . "

Marta really likes the word "why." I don't. I know her well. We've been together for four years. I let her keep talking, get it all out, in order to avoid answering her questions. Oh, it may be a cliché, but with women it always works. And then this time I have no choice, I'm obliged to keep silent, because I'm bound by state secrets. The end of every conversation with Marta is always the same:

"Christian, do you love me?"

"Of course I love you."

"Christian, you're the love of my life!"

Afterward I call my family. That goes smoothly. No worries. By now they're used to my travels, or maybe they know that in

Tunis I'm as comfortable as in my own home, so they're not worried about anything. I have time to telephone my two sisters and my brother for a quick hello.

Captain Judas arrives. We have a coffee before setting to work on Al Qaeda's Web threats against Italy. I take advantage of the calm to attempt an intervention.

"Can I ask you a favor?"

"What do you need, Tunisian?"

"Can you help Mohamed get his residency permit?"

"Who might this Mohammed be?"

"My Moroccan fellow-tenant."

"What sort of request is that, Tunisian? Have you forgotten the goal of your mission?"

"No, I haven't forgotten anything."

"Instead of uncovering terrorists you're turning into a social worker. Congratulations!"

"I'm doing as much as I can."

"It's not enough!"

I listen reluctantly to the captain's scolding. By now I know his words by heart, like: "The terrorists are ready to strike in Rome"; "All hell's about to break loose, worse than the attacks in New York or Madrid." Or: "We're playing in the final seconds." The absolute worst is this: "You'll make me look like shit to my American and Egyptian colleagues." They all want results, and now.

Maybe he just needs to vent. I should put myself in his shoes. He's under heavy pressure from his superiors. He's in the line of fire and if something goes wrong he'll pay. But really, I'm doing as much as I can. What else can I do?

Anyway, before we say goodbye he promises he'll intervene to solve Mohammed's problem. Can I trust an officer in the secret service who, besides, is named Judas? We'll see!

SOFIA

I wake up every day at six, and by now I'm used to this rhythm. I don't need the alarm clock. The architect, on the other hand, sleeps until noon. Monday is his day off. In Italy a lot of restaurants are closed on the first day of the week. Apart from Monday his schedule is always the same: he goes to work at four and comes home after twelve-thirty, eats, watches the Arabic satellite channels (especially Madame Al Jazeera) until dawn, then goes to sleep. He doesn't miss anything, because there are repeats. He is very well informed when it comes to international affairs, such as the war in Iraq, the Iranian nuclear program, Hezbollah, Hamas, etc. If you heard him speak on these subjects you would say without hesitation that he is not a pizza maker but an analyst in some institute for strategic studies. In other words, he could be the U.N. Secretary General's envoy to the Middle East. He has all the necessary qualifications.

About what happens in Italy, on the contrary, he knows almost nothing. His theory is very simple: if Al Jazeera doesn't talk about it, that means that nothing important happens here. He's always instructing me not to trust the Italian media. Why? Because they discuss Islam in a negative way: a religion of hatred and violence that can only incite holy war. All Muslims are fanatical terrorists, ready to blow themselves up without a second thought.

I don't agree with the architect. I've often told him that he's making a big mistake. When you live in a country, you should give precedence to the local news. For example, I find the local news on RAI 3 really interesting because it gives me a lot of useful information about Rome and the surrounding area. I want to know how things are here in Rome, not in Kabul or Baghdad. You see?

The satellite channels have become real traps for the Arab immigrants. They create a dependence on one's native country. How can you live split between two countries? I can't follow the daily news of Italy and the Arab world at the same time. You have to choose. It's not that complicated, or am I wrong?

I have a lot of free time during the day, because I don't work. I am, as they say, a housewife. I do my best not to get bored. Time is something precious, and I always find something worthwhile to do. In the morning I finish the cleaning quickly and spend a couple of hours studying Italian. I'm self-taught; I learned the language on my own—I never took a course. I often use the dictionary to understand the meaning of difficult words, and I have a notebook where I write down new words. Thank God I have a talent for languages and a personal method for learning. I place enormous importance on pronunciation. To speak a language well you have to practice it. This is fundamental. I listen to Italian radio and watch the television channels to get my ear used to the musicality of the words. Italian is the most musical language. There's always something to learn. I hardly ever watch the Arab channels; they're unbearable because of the amount of politics and soap operas.

As an Egyptian, I grew up with homemade soap operas. The Brazilian, Mexican, and Turkish ones came much later. Thanks to the satellite, they've had a wide circulation. Over time, I got fed up with them. I said enough of these tearjerker shows. The scripts always had (and still do have, alas) the same ingredients: a man and a woman (one of the two has to be starving) love each other, but they can't crown their love with marriage. Usually, it's the rich family that gets in the way. The two main characters do their utmost to resist, and to overcome all the obstacles. In the last episode, they triumph: she in her white dress and he in a suit and tie. And they lived happily ever after, as Scheherazade says at the end of her stories in the *Thousand and One Nights*.

I often get compliments on how well I speak Italian. I've been mistaken for an Italian who has converted to Islam or for someone who was born in Italy or came here as a child. And so? So what. I like it when people don't stop at my veil but look beyond it. Still going on about the damn veil? No, I have no intention of talking about the veil, at least right now. Later on we'll see.

Anyway, my daughter, Aida, is very good, like me, while her father is a real disaster: like many Egyptians he can't pronounce "p." A "b" is dragged into its place. You can imagine the result. You want a taste? No problem. Here's a short sketch. The setting is Little Cairo. On the stage are two actors: Said Ahmed Metwalli alias Felice alias my husband and another orphan of the letter "p." The dialogue is strictly in Italian, no subtitles or dubbing.

"My friend, too much time has bassed. What a bleasure to see you."

"The bleasure is mine."

"Where have you been, Barma?"

"Not Barma, Baris. I went there to work."

"Still a bizza maker?"

"Yes, I'm really an exbert at bizza."

"Tell me, you still do the brayer?"

"Of course, brayer is very imbortant. Second billar of Islam."

"Combliments. You're a true bracticing Muslim."

"And how are you?"

"Today not well, I've got stomach broblems."

"Why? What did you have for lunch?"

"Chicken and botatoes, but too sbicy."

"You boor thing."

"The stomach is like a wife, never leaves you in beace."

"You've got it berfectly right. Hahaha."

The finale is amusing. Remarks by husbands about wives always work. They'll give you a good laugh, provided they're made to men.

Aida is four, and she speaks both Arabic and Italian well. She's very quick. I'm her teacher. Since I don't have a job (I mean officially), it didn't make sense to enroll her in a nursery school. And then finding a place takes a miracle. The schools are all full. The birth rate in Italy is the lowest in Europe, and you still need a lot of connections to get a place. In this way, Italy isn't very different from the Arab countries and the third world: nepotism is a widespread practice. Thank God there are immigrant women who continue to have children in spite of the problems they face. So? So what. I see a lot of old people, and in the parks there are more dogs than children! In the future, God only knows what will happen. Is Italy becoming a country without children?

I often listen to the radio while I'm cleaning the house. This morning on one of the RAI channels there were two experts talking about Islamic terrorism. I was really struck by a statement one of them made: "The root of the evil is inherent in an Islam that is physiologically violent and historically marked by conflict. The real problem is that Muslims don't know what love is." The other comments: "But Christians, Jews, and Hindus have also used violence in the name of religion. For us Catholics it's enough to remember the Inquisition in the Middle Ages."

I keep repeating to myself this phrase: Muslims don't know what love is. It's a heavy sentence, without appeal. It means that we are animals, barbarians, inhuman! In other words, people who have no right to live. I turn off the radio and put on a CD of Om Kalthoum, the singer of love. The song is called *Enta omri*, "You Are My Life."

Your eyes have brought me back to the days that are gone
They have taught me to regret the past and its wounds.

Around ten I take Aida to the park in Piazza Meucci so she can play with the other children. Outside the house she likes calling me Sofia and not mamma. In the park I meet other young mothers, and we start chatting about this and that.

I sit down next to Giulia, a Roman woman I've known for two years. We've become friends. She works part time in a real-estate agency. She's thirty-eight and has a lively little boy. She often talks about the difficulties of having a child in Italy. If you don't have parents behind you—and they have to be in good health, too—you won't get anywhere. She's always saying, "In Italy you either have a job or have kids, the two together never work out." Many women, especially those employed as freelance workers, lose their jobs as soon as they go on maternity leave. They have no security. Giulia regrets the disappearance of the extended family, which made life less stressful, because the child care was divided among grandparents, aunts, cousins . . .

Giulia isn't married, but she lives with the man who is the father of her son. She never calls him her husband, but her companion. She's not a wife but a companion. They live under the same roof and share the same bed, yet they're not married! It's a situation that's rather complicated for an Egyptian Muslim like me to understand. Of course, I'm not stupid. When people explain things to me I understand. I have to admit that the problem is not in understanding but in accepting. Does companion mean friend or not? A husband is one thing, a friend another. And so? So what. In other words, in between there's a sexual relationship, or am I wrong? It's not unimportant. The truth is that I can't put myself in her place: I can't imagine liv-

ing with a man, and also having a child by him, without marriage. For me it's impossible. In Islam it's called *zina*, adultery,
and is severely punished. In this case there's no difference in
how a man and a woman are treated: a hundred lashes if the
two guilty ones are unmarried. If they're already married the
punishment is stoning, which is an atrocious death. These cor-
poral punishments are applied in Iran and a few other countries. In Egypt, and in the majority of Muslim countries, the set
punishment is jail. A child born outside of marriage is called *ibn
zina*, the child of adultery. Society will consider him not a victim but rather an accomplice in a very serious crime.

Giulia has explained to me many times why couples prefer
living together to marriage. The percentage of divorce in Italy
is very high. Every year people marry less and divorce more.
Before settling down with someone, you have to seriously consider the possibility of divorce. Then, there's another important element: divorce is very expensive in Italy, because of the
bureaucracy. Most people who get divorced have to spend a lot
of money, plus they have to wait at least three years.

In the Muslim religion divorce is very quick. Two words are
enough to sanction it: *Anti tàliq*, I divorce you! That is the formula for divorce. Usually it's the man who has this power. The
third time the words are uttered the divorce becomes final.
After the first two times, it's possible to reconcile, but after the
third it gets a little more complicated. If the ex-husband wants
to go back to the ex-wife, he has to marry her again. Exactly.
But that's not all; there's another condition, or, rather, three.
First, the ex-wife has to marry another man, who obviously has
to be a Muslim (no Christians, Jews, Buddhists, and so forth),
and the marriage has to be consummated. Only under these
conditions can she then divorce and remarry her ex-husband.
Clear? Not very.

O.K., I see the difficulty of explaining the matter to non-
Muslims. I'll try to be more explicit, but it means I have to talk

about my private life. Unfortunately I myself have had experience of these unpleasant things. In five years of marriage, my husband and I have already passed the second divorce. In other words, my husband has already pronounced the formula for divorce twice. Both circumstances are vivid to me. Both times it had to do with arguments. The first goes back to a couple of years ago. We quarreled because I insisted on working as a babysitter. The second is more recent, and the reason is more serious. He wanted to have another child right away, and I didn't. I needed to reflect before making such an important decision. My husband is a good person, but he has one big fault: he loses control easily. When he gets angry, he's like a drunk, or rather a wild dog. Anyway, after the first and the second divorce he apologized, weeping. In both cases he admitted his mistakes. And what could I do? I agreed to let Imam Zaki mediate; he acted as a peacemaker, because he's like a brother to me. In Cairo we lived in the same neighborhood, and his sister was a childhood friend of mine. I was thinking mainly of my daughter's future. After the second divorce, Imam Zaki was very severe with the architect. He told him that divorce isn't a game. He lingered a long time on the meaning of a quotation from the Prophet: "Among licit acts the most hated by God is divorce." In the end he gave him a warning: "Look out, you're playing with fire—the next divorce will be final." Usually I try to listen to the imam's words without commenting. But this time I couldn't. "I'm certainly not the one who's asking for a divorce, so the one responsible is him and him alone." I said it in a tone of exasperation.

Now I don't want to think about the third divorce, and especially its consequences. I believe deeply in *maktùb*, so I look to the future serenely and without worrying too much. And then the right to divorce in Islam is not exclusively the man's; the woman can have it, too, in the rare cases where she is stronger in the marriage negotiations.

There's one question that goes around and around in my head, and I can't get rid of it. Why can a Muslim man marry a Christian or a Jew whereas a Muslim woman can't marry either a Christian or a Jew? The five pillars of Islam are valid for both men and women. So why shouldn't all have the same rights and the same duties?

After twenty minutes Dorina, our Albanian friend, joined us. She's a Muslim like me but she doesn't wear a veil. She's the caretaker for Giovanni, an old man who has a lot of trouble walking. Dorina is twenty-nine and has lived in Rome for six years. She has a really terrible story. I'll try to summarize it. She's nineteen, living peacefully with her family in Tirana. She dreams of going to the university and studying medicine. One dark day she meets a handsome young man who courts her persistently, saying he's madly in love with her and wants to marry her. Dorina trusts him, falls in love, especially when the young man officially asks for her hand (a soap opera Albanian style?). After a couple of months she agrees to go on vacation with him in Italy. From that moment the romantic dream turns into a nightmare. Dorina discovers the truth: the fiancé is a ruthless criminal who uses the promise of marriage as bait to lure beautiful girls into his trap. Dorina is sold as a slave to a criminal gang and forced to work as a prostitute. After four years of torture she finds the courage to report her exploiters, with the help of an organization that fights the prostitution racket preying on immigrant girls. So she gets her residency permit and moves to Rome to change her life. She has never gone back to Albania because she's ashamed, she's afraid of how people will react, and also that her exploiters might take revenge. Now Dorina hates men, all men, and she often cries when she recalls freezing nights waiting for clients on the out-skirts of all those cities. I always try to cheer her up.

Grandfather Giovanni is over eighty, and has some hearing problems. But in my opinion he's not quite right in the head.

He usually sits on a bench, the same one, reading *La Padania, Libero*, and *Il Giornale*. You're in trouble if you disturb him, even just to ask the time. You have to leave him alone. After he finishes reading, he bursts out with comments like: "I hope I die before Romania enters the European Union"; "Soon we'll be invaded by the Gypsies, they're like locusts, and we'll have migrant camps everywhere, even right outside our houses"; "What's the government waiting for to close all the mosques and throw the Muslims in jail?"; "If the Muslim immigrants really want to assimilate, they should convert and become Catholics! I want to see them at Sunday Mass!"; "Damn Communists. It's always their fault." The finale is almost always the same: "Oh, my country, so beautiful and so lost!"

Grandfather Giovanni calls me "sister." I've told him over and over, "I'm not a nun, I'm a Muslim." And he answers, "What? You dress like the sisters and you're not a sister?" I try to persuade him: "I can't be a sister, I have a husband and a child." And he: "I see, the Muslims are mad for women. They even marry sisters!" I don't have the least desire to explain to him that nuns don't exist in Islam and that the Prophet Mohammed strongly advised against monasticism. Among us people say, "Marriage is half religion," or "Marriage is prevention." Many transgressions are linked to sins of the flesh, to sex. When someone marries it becomes easier to hold temptation at bay. But perhaps this applies more to men than to us women, or am I wrong?

Once Grandfather Giovanni made me practically die laughing. After the usual reading of the newspapers he stared at me for ten seconds or so, then he fired off questions like a high-speed train.

"*Libero* says that the Americans are resigned: they won't get bin Laden alive or dead. Excuse me, sister, I would like to ask you a question."

"Please, Signor Giovanni."

"This damn bin Laden, where is he hiding?"

"I don't know."

"What do you mean you don't know, sister? He can't have disappeared into thin air. Have you hidden him somewhere, the way you did with Saddam Hussein?"

"I'm sorry, I don't know anything about it."

"All right, all right. You don't trust me because I don't belong to your religion. You know, I was in the war, so I'm an expert in military matters. You see, I have a hypothesis on bin Laden's hiding place."

"Really?"

"Bin Laden is a Saudi, right?"

"Right."

"So he's hiding in Mecca, in that square mausoleum you call Ka . . . Ka . . . Kamikaze or . . . Kawasaki."

Fantastic! An ingenious hypothesis. The Kaaba, built by Abraham, has become a motorcycle brand! But poor Giovanni is only a parrot, he repeats the stupid things he reads in the papers. Luckily he's almost deaf. Every cloud has a silver lining! What garbage would come out of that mouth if he could follow the programs on TV and radio.

Before going to the market to do the shopping I stop off at the Marconi library to borrow a book or a movie. The staff are all women, who are polite and kind. I choose a book of fairy tales for Aida. Then I go up to the second floor to glance at the newspapers. I see the young man with the tissue, the Arab without a name. I pretend not to notice him. He is looking at me.

Around noon I go home to make lunch. After we eat, the architect plants himself in front of the TV for another round with Al Jazeera. Sometimes I think of Al Jazeera as a real rival, a sort of daytime lover. He spends more time with her than with me. And so? So what. Maybe I'm starting to become a jealous wife. Should I be worried?

At four my husband leaves the house to go to work. The

second part of my free time begins. I take Aida and go to see Samira, my best friend. We live in the same building—all I have to do is go down one floor. For me she's like a big sister. Samira is Algerian; she's ten years older than I am, and has lived in Rome for fifteen years. She's married to a Tunisian truck driver, and she has three children. She's a housewife, but she doesn't wear the veil. I met her when I arrived in Rome. We became friends immediately, and now we see each other practically every day, usually in the afternoon. We tell each other everything and we give each other a ton of advice. I often leave Aida with her when I have pressing things to do.

At eight I go home. After dinner I put my daughter to bed with a story. I'm not sleepy, so I decide to watch TV. I take a quick tour of the channels, using the remote. Nothing interesting on the Italian ones. So I try the Arabic. On a Lebanese channel I find a classic film with the legendary singer Abdel Halim Hafez and the actress Meriem Fakhr Eddine. It's a love story about a young aspiring singer, desperately poor, and a beautiful rich girl. Soap-opera stuff? No, not at all. It's a romantic movie with fabulous songs. It reminds me of my adolescence. I was in love, too. With whom? With a doctor, but he was married and had children. It was a platonic love, consisting of looks and a lot of fantasies. I've seen this film a bunch of times. I know all the details. Here's my favorite scene. The two lovers are on the banks of the Nile. It's night, the stars are out, Abdel Halim sings to his beloved *Belumuni leh*?, why do you criticize me?

Why do you criticize me?
If you, too, could see
Her eyes, so beautiful you could die,
It would seem to you right that I think only of her
And can no longer sleep.

ISSA

The other day Mohammed the Moroccan received a strange phone call from the Rome police headquarters. He was told to appear the following day to receive his residency permit. He thought they were pulling his leg, but it was true. He woke at dawn so he'd be punctual for the appointment, assuming he'd have to wait in the usual long line for non-Europeans.

As soon as the office opened he went in to make inquiries. The agent, sitting behind a window with a tired and irritated look, merely entered the name in the computer. As he waited for the response Mohammed was very worried. Apart from that blasted telephone call, he had nothing, not a single scrap of paper with an official stamp, to bring as proof. Appointments are serious. You can't just show up empty-handed. That's how things work at police headquarters, commissioners' offices, and checkpoints in airports. And Mohammed knows this very well, because he's been in Italy since the eighties. Over time he has also developed a system of defense against possible reactions of police and municipal and postal employees, their use of the familiar *tu* rather than the formal *lei*, the sarcastic expressions, the ironic smiles, the provocative questions . . .

This time, however, it was different. The policeman said, with a big, broad smile, "Signor Mohammed, they are expecting you in the diplomatic office. Here, take your pass." He couldn't believe his ears. It was too strange. It seemed to him a sort of *Candid Camera* featuring not celebs but poor immigrants. Maybe he let slip to himself some comment like "What's happening to me?" or "Bastards, they're making fun of me," or "I'm only dreaming and soon I'm going to wake up." In short, he needed time to get used to words like "signor," "diplomatic office," and "pass," since people in his category generally never heard them. You can't change like that, point blank.

In the waiting room, he sat beside people with connections, people who count, the crème de la crème: families of foreign ambassadors in Italy, Russian and Chinese entrepreneurs, first-class non-Europeans (Americans and Canadians). He got a headache that lasted for the rest of the day. He felt out of place in every sense. And in the end he was issued a residency permit valid for two years. Until that moment he had been living in the nightmare of receiving a permit that was already expired. Now he could enjoy two years of peace.

Mohammed was still in shock. He couldn't find any explanation for the phone call from the police and the warm welcome they had given him. He continued to speak of an inexplicable miracle. A providential intervention. He didn't know whom to thank. God? Maybe, because last year he had observed Ramadan. His mother? Maybe, because he always prays for her.

I would have liked to reveal to Mohammed the true identity of his guardian angel, but I couldn't. State secret.

I get in line for the bathroom. Luckily it's not long. I dress quickly to go to the café for my usual morning cappuccino. Saber asks me to wait because he wants to tell me something important. Will he talk to me about Simona Barberini or about the Milan team? We'll see. In five minutes we're going out together. With him now I speak only Italian, I mean his Italian, with the "b" in place of the "p."

"I've got something imbortant to tell you."

"What?"

"There's a sby among us."

"A spy?"

"Yes, the bastard will be uncovered soon. We'll bust his ass."

"Who is it?"

"We have a susbect, but broof is lacking."

"And who does he work for?"

"For that fucking whore Teresa."

Shit, I practically had a heart attack! Worse, I was peeing in my pants. That would be the least of it in the face of this god-damn suspense. Saber explains that the "rat" has been employed by the landlady alias Vacation for a long time. So she knows about everything that happens here. The most serious thing has to do with the visitors who sleep in the kitchen. My fellow-tenants are afraid that Teresa will exploit this business to increase the number of beds, by adding a bunk bed to every room. She can come to us and say tranquilly, "My dear immigrant Muslims, you see? Sixteen of you can live happily and comfortably." So she would have a new source of income, of four or five hundred euros a month. The hypothesis can't be ruled out, given all the ads for exotic tours and low-cost cruises you see these days. More and more, this apartment resembles an overcrowded prison. The good news is that there's another spy, although his duties are different from mine. In other words, a new colleague so I won't feel alone. To each his mission. Hooray!

On the way to Little Cairo I get a text message from Judas. He wants to see me right away. Usually we meet in the afternoon. Why has he changed the plan? It takes me twenty minutes to get to Via Nazionale. Judas opens the door and asks me to follow him out onto the balcony to talk. He grabs a cigarette but doesn't light it right away. During these weeks I've started getting to know him: when he's nervous he prefers to stand up, preferably outside. Why does he do it? Probably to avoid the gaze of his interlocutor. He stands there and pretends to look at the passersby, the trees, the cars. A perfect way to hide his own emotions. To break the ice, I tell him about Mohammed's adventure at the police station. He listens without saying a word. In fact he seems really annoyed.

"Anyway, I'd like to thank you for your help at police headquarters."

"You're happy for your Moroccan friend?"

"Of course—he was getting really depressed."

"Wonderful! We've become two fine social workers. Instead of uncovering terrorists we're saving immigrant workers from depression. In short, we're just as good as Caritas volunteers!"

"Why did you want to see me?"

"To give you some good news."

"What?"

"Dear Tunisian, your new friends in Viale Marconi are about to fuck us in a big way."

"What do you mean?"

"We've received some disturbing information. In recent days fifty kilos of Goma-2 Eco have arrived in Rome, the same explosive used in the attacks in Madrid."

"Shit!"

"We're looking for corroboration. If the information is confirmed we wouldn't have time to stop them."

We don't say much because there's not much to say. The situation is serious. I return to Viale Marconi distressed and terrified. The scenes of the victims of the slaughter in Madrid pass before my eyes without interruption. Something has to be done to stop the attackers. But what?

In the afternoon I go to Little Cairo. Every day I follow the same script. I call Tunis, and a woman's voice answers, but not "mamma"'s. "Hello, little brother, it's Amel." It's my "sister," the pregnant one. It won't be hard to talk. And in fact we devote the whole conversation to the baby. First of all, they have to find a name. Discussions are under way, but there is no shortage of problems. If it's a girl her husband wants to give her the name of her dead grandmother. My "sister" is not totally in agreement.

"You think it's right to give a child born in 2005 the name Saadia?"

"Certainly it's not a fashionable name today."

"I have no doubt of its great merit, since it refers to the woman who acted as mother to the Prophet Mohammed when he was orphaned. But should we look to the future or to the past?"

"The future."

"See? You think the way I do. You wouldn't call your daughter Saadia, either!"

The list of objections is extremely long. My "sister" is convinced that if the daughter (damn, she's not even born yet) is named Saadia she'll have an inferiority complex all her life and never find a husband. Poor Saadia won't be able to compete with the Jessicas, Pamelas, Samanthas, Isabellas, etc. The Brazilian and Mexican soap operas are endless sources of names of all types and for all tastes. It's just an embarrassment of choices.

My "sister," for instance, is very fond of the name Maria. Her husband is against it because he considers it a Christian name. She defends it energetically by pointing out that one of the wives of our Prophet was named Maria: she may have been a Copt, but she converted to Islam. So there would be no religious transgression—it would be in full obedience to tradition. The situation is serious. Is the marriage really in the balance? Don't be ridiculous. Anyway, we hope that the newborn will be male so we can avoid this mess. I say goodbye to my "sister" Amel after the usual stream of advice for a pregnant woman, and I go to pay for the phone call. Waiting for the news on Al Jazeera I start talking to an Egyptian about the war in Iraq. My companion, a graduate in international relations, explains to me that the Americans' objective is not to democratize Iraq but to destabilize Syria and, especially, Iran. What a grand discovery! Every knows it, even the camels of the Sahara. I pretend to listen to his analysis, every so often throwing out an observation or a brief comment. I don't want to be taken for an idiot with nothing to say. In other words, it's a two-way conversation, not a one-way lesson.

Anyway, I am open to all conversation, from politics to sports, from economics to history, from archeology to medicine. I'm ready to talk to anyone. The important thing is to socialize with as many people as possible. I try to play the part of a friendly young immigrant, carefree and outgoing, who likes to be with people.

At a certain point I take my eyes off the television screen, I look around, and who do I see? The girl with the veil. Luckily this time she's not crying, in fact she's smiling. She's even prettier than before, with that colored veil. As she goes out, I try to photograph her in my memory. I even manage to see the cover of the CD she has in her hands: Om Kalthoum's *Awedt Einy*, "I'm Used to Seeing You." I decide not to follow her. I'm here on a very particular mission. I've got to get busy and try to find out the members of this damn second terrorist cell.

So far I've bought a lot of coffees and teas for quite a number of Arabs in order to grease the wheels of friendship. I have to say that I've done pretty well. The Egyptians are like Neapolitans: they know how to make themselves agreeable, or at least they make an effort; sometimes they succeed, sometimes they don't. Certainly, they are incurable exhibitionists; they never want to go unnoticed. So they're a bit touchy when they don't receive the right amount of attention. With me they have no problems: I guarantee total concentration on what they have to say. They're never tired of seducing you, above all with words. When they use Egyptian Arabic, which is known in the whole Arab world, thanks to the soap operas, they seem like consummate actors. A Tunisian girl once said to me, "Egyptians are never spontaneous, they always seems to be playing a part, with the script in their hand." She's right. They're nothing like the Maghrebi. It's hard for Middle Eastern Arabs to understand the Arabic of Moroccans, Tunisians, and Algerians

I have to interrupt my conversation with the Egyptian about democracy and the war in Iraq—Akram alias John Belushi is calling me.

"Tunisian!"

"Yes?"

"Are you still looking for work?"

"Yes."

"Inshallah, there's something for you. You want to wash dishes?"

Fantastic! A job possibility. I've done well to hang out here every damn day. Little Cairo is a strategic place. So many people come and go, as a result they exchange information of every type: apartments, jobs, possible legalization for illegals, couples in crisis, imminent marriages and divorces, and so on. Akram is really clever—he manages to intercept all this flow and use it to his advantage to augment his "commercial" power. My compliments!

The Egyptian explains that the dishwasher job is available immediately, so it would be smart to begin today. Then, it has one great plus: the restaurant is very close to Piazza della Radio. Sleeping over the store, so to speak: I won't have spend hours waiting for the night bus. The crucial thing is to stay in the neighborhood, not get too far from Viale Marconi. Finally he advises me to go to the restaurant right away and ask for his friend the Egyptian pizza maker, the architect Felice. But what sort of name is that? And then, what the hell is an architect doing in a pizzeria!

"Tunisian, I've found you a home and a job."

"Thank you, *hagg* Akram."

"Now if you want I can find you a wife."

"No, thanks. Mamma's already taking care of it."

"It's time to give you a push. Remember that marriage is the goal of Islam."

I thank Akram with a strong handshake. I get the directions and go to the restaurant without wasting any time. The place is nearby, and I arrive in a few minutes. I ask for the pizza maker, Felice. He's just arrived.

"My name is Said, but here they call me Felice, my nom de guerre. Hahaha."

"Nice to meet you, I'm Issa."

"Akram spoke well of you. He said you're O.K. In other words, different from the other Tunisians, who deal drugs."

"Each of us is responsible for what he does."

"Right."

I don't pay much attention to the stereotype of the Tunisian drug dealer. I was inoculated long ago against these shitty prejudices: the Sicilian Mafioso, the Neapolitan Camorrist, the Sardinian kidnapper, the Albanian criminal, the Gypsy thief, the Muslim terrorist, and so on and on. In Arabic Said means *felice*, happy. So it can't be said that he has changed his name—he's just found the corresponding Italian. Felice offers me coffee and we exchange a little information. He's lived in Italy for twelve years, and has an architecture degree from the University of Cairo. That's why they call him *bashmohandes*, architect. He still harbors dreams of someday practicing his profession. He's married and has a small daughter. From the way he speaks, I understand that he's very observant. He's constantly quoting verses from the Koran and sayings of the Prophet. He's like an imam. The arrival of the restaurant owner, a guy named Damiano, who's around sixty, compels us to interrupt our pleasant chat. Felice introduces me, saying I'm a respectable young man. And now the job interview, or, rather, the interrogation.

"Where are you from?"

"I'm from Tunisia."

"You speak Italian?"

"Yes."

"You have documents?"

"Yes."

"What's your name?"

"Issa."

"Why do you all have strange names? What does it mean?"

"It's the name of Jesus in Arabic."

"So you're Christian?"

"No, Muslim."

"You're a Muslim and you're called Jesus! I continue not to understand a fucking thing about you Muslims. Have you worked in a restaurant before?"

"No."

"Don't worry, it doesn't matter. I just want boys who are serious, and on time, and don't bug me. Understand?"

"Yes."

"As you see, I'm not a racist. I don't discriminate between Muslims and Christians, people with a residency permit and illegals. For me they're all the same. Understand?"

"Yes."

"Listen, I've already forgotten your name. It's hard to remember. We'll have to call you something else, what do you prefer: Christian or Tunisian?"

Obviously I choose the second. A Muslim who is called Christian is pure provocation. It would be like going to Mecca with a cross around your neck. I don't have the slightest intention of running that risk.

I begin work right away, after accepting the owner's conditions: two weeks' trial and forget about a contract; that is, I work illegally from opening till closing. I think of my residency permit, so far it's been of no help either for renting the bed or for the job. Who knows, maybe it will turn out to be useful for wiping my ass when I can't find toilet paper.

In the kitchen I meet the three cooks: two Bangladeshis and a Peruvian. Besides Felice there's an Egyptian pizza assistant named Farid. The waiters, on the other hand, are all Italians. The customers have no contact with the immigrant staff. Is it a coincidence?

I finish work around two in the morning. Everyone has left except the boss, who is enjoying a last whiskey before going to bed. It will take some time to get used to the fact that among the duties of the dishwasher are the cleaning of the kitchen and the two bathrooms. In short, I'm also the housewife of the restaurant.

I go home dead tired. I fall sleep without any problem. The insomnia of the past few days seems to have disappeared by itself. I begin to understand something important: people who work hard don't need sleeping pills to get their sleep. Those are for the rich, who don't do shit from morning to evening. The usual war between rich and poor. *"Cu avi suonnu nun cerca capizzu"*—"When you're tired you don't go looking for a pillow." This is called class conflict. Am I becoming a Communist? Don't be ridiculous. It's just the delirium of exhaustion.

SOFIA

I'm sitting across from the Trevi fountain. It's the middle of the night and no one is around. I see the big blonde (the one from *La Dolce Vita*) in the fountain, under the waterfall. Suddenly she starts shouting, in English, "Marcello, come here!" I go on watching, but I'm blinded by jealousy. Marcello Mastroianni is sitting there having coffee and he doesn't make a move. I can't bear it for very long, I take off my scarf and walk into the fountain. The water is freezing. Marcello puts aside his cup of coffee and gets up. I'm very surprised, because he's looking not at the blonde but at me. I'm flattered. After a while he approaches. And when our gazes meet I realize that Marcello has the face of the guy with the tissue (the Arab without a name) whom I met first at Little Cairo and then at the Marconi library. After that I begin to tremble with cold. The Arab Marcello (from now on I'll call him that) immediately understands that and embraces me very sweetly. I'm so happy. But the dream ends and abruptly I wake up.

Thank God I remember my dreams clearly, from beginning to end. And so? So what. I won't have any trouble telling Samira. She is great at interpreting dreams—she always manages to get something important out of them. She often says, "The dream is an inner voice that comes directly from the heart."

I get through the housecleaning in a hurry. Around ten-thirty I leave my husband sleeping soundly, as I do every morning, and go with Aida to the park in Piazza Meucci. When I get there I find Giulia and Dorina sitting on a bench chatting. Near them are two children playing on the swing, and Aida runs off to join them. Grandfather Giovanni is totally immersed in his newspaper. How strange! He's reading *Il Manifesto!* What has happened in the world? Has he become a Communist? Why has he given up *Padania, Libero*, and *Il Giornale*? Life is strange. Nothing lasts forever, except God Almighty. I prefer not to say hello to him, in order not to disturb him. His reactions are always unpredictable.

I sit beside my two friends. I quickly discover the subject of discussion. Today we're talking about breasts. About preventing breast cancer? No, about cosmetic surgery. Now that voluptuous bosoms are fashionable, many women (often they're still adolescents, I've heard that the operation can even be a gift for high-school graduation) decide to remake their breasts in order to appear beautiful, attractive, or simply sexier. Giulia and Dorina are in favor of the operation. Giulia says, "What's wrong with it? Today going to the cosmetic surgeon is like going to the dentist or the gynecologist." Dorina agrees, "We live in 2005. A woman should be free to dispose of her own body as she likes."

I myself have a different opinion, and since it's impossible for me to remain silent, I have to interrupt to defend my convictions. My theory is simple: veils are not always pieces of fabric, there are tricks, comparable to our veil, that hide other parts of the body. And so? So what. In other words, the reshaped breast hides the original breast, the reshaped nose hides the original nose, the reshaped lips hide the original lips, and so on. I begin my sermon (I'm a good orator, one day I might even become a female imam!) with the health risks: how many poor breasts are ruined by operations? Unfortunately I don't have statistics at hand, but the percentage of failures is high. Dorina and Giulia (now they're speaking with a single voice) reply, "The cosmetic surgeon is a doctor like any other doctor, so it happens that every so often he makes a mistake.

These are things that happen in every field of medicine." On this point they're not wrong. The medical argument won't get me anywhere. I have to change my strategy and find something more persuasive.

I move to religion, a subject I know better; in other words, I'm still a believing and practicing Muslim. So the question is this: what is the position of Islam on cosmetic surgery? It is *haram*, illegal, if the surgery is not indispensable. Which means? If a person gets a broken nose in a car accident and can no longer breathe well he has every right to turn to a cosmetic surgeon to fix it. Here beauty has nothing to do with it. It's a matter of health. Clear? Instead, if a woman looks at herself in the mirror when she wakes up in the morning and decides to touch up her upper lip because she doesn't like it anymore, Islam says, "No, madame. You can't." Why? The reason is simple: our body doesn't belong to us—the true owner is God Almighty. When we're born we take it only in trust, it's under our management for a limited time. In the end we have to give it back in good condition. Even tattoos are *haram*.

Dorina and Giulia listen to me with interest. I understand that my speech has hit the mark. I've got one line left before the curtain falls. You have to leave the stage in grand style and to applause. So here comes the finale. "Excuse me! What will a reshaped woman say to God Almighty on Judgment Day? I'm giving back the body that I had on loan. But . . . I'm sorry . . . the breast surgery didn't go well."

Giulia stares at me a moment before moving to the counterattack. "Judgment Day? What are you talking about, Sofia? You know what I say? I don't give a damn about Islam, I'm not a Muslim. Well, all right, I'm a Catholic who remembers I'm a Catholic only at Christmas and Easter. In reality I'm allergic to all religions, without exception. I'll do what I like with my body. Do you understand?"

Giulia's words make a breach in the silence of our Albanian

friend. "I don't deny that I'm a Muslim, but in my private life I want to be free: my body belongs only to me. We say that God gave it to me. All right? And we can do what we want with this gift, or not? Otherwise what sort of gift would it be?"

Bravo Dorina! Solid reasoning, really. I'd never thought of the body as a divine gift. Anyway, the religious argument wasn't a great idea for the case against cosmetic surgery. I'm an observant believer and I act accordingly. For Dorina and Giulia the situation is completely different. Let's say they're sailing in other seas.

To what point can we Muslims consider ourselves truly free? While I reflect on the meaning of freedom in Islam, Giulia won't let go—she wants to have the last word. "Dear Sofia, you wear the veil, so you don't need to show off a shapely bosom. Think of poor women like us, who can't display a nice décolleté because of their flat chests, and so they get complexes." And Dorina in support: "Who would ever have said? Even the veil has its advantages. You're lucky, Sofia." Me, lucky? Well, maybe, yes. Basically, why always be complaining? Dorina is very ironic. But I'm not joking, either, and when I start there's trouble for everybody. "You want to wear the veil, like me? No problem. Please, make yourself comfortable. Welcome to the club of veiled women."

More laughs.

Grandfather Giovanni, sitting on the bench next to ours, comes out of his isolation. Maybe we've disturbed him. He has the look of an angry person. Is he mad at us? It's likely. He stares at us for a few seconds, then throws the paper on the ground, shouting, "Have you seen what those Communist bastards of the *Manifesto* write? They say that the partisans are heroes, patriots, the country's saviors! I say they are a band of traitors. Yes, they are trai-*tors*. The ones who are still alive should be hanged and I spit on the graves of the dead. Goddamn Communists!"

Giulia explains this business of the partisans. Kind of complicated, to tell the truth. They are heroes because they fought the Nazis to liberate the country from the occupation, and traitors because they murdered the leader Benito Mussolini. It's really hard to have a clear and definite opinion. Today Grandfather Giovanni is in a terrible mood. Dorina tells us the reason. The old man gets depressed because, ever since his wife died, three years ago, he's felt abandoned by his children. They come to see him only on big occasions. When he wants to express his sadness he buys the *Manifesto* and pretends to read it. Then he vents his feelings by getting angry at the partisans. It's a simple trick, but it always works. Dorina decides to intervene right away and takes the old man home before the situation gets worse. You never know. Giulia, too, leaves after a few minutes.

The time passes quickly, it's almost lunchtime. I have to go to the market to do the shopping. I like to wander among the fruit and vegetable stalls. Shopping is a career, in fact an art, as my father always says. There are important rules to follow. First, examine the goods very patiently. Second, don't respond immediately to the solicitations of the vendors. Third, take the time necessary to choose what you want. Fourth, buy exclusively on the basis of the quality-price relationship. You have to be like a good hunter: strike at the right moment in order not to make a mistake. Maybe I've found my prey. This vendor has the best apples in the market. There are two people ahead of me. After a couple of minutes it's my turn. As I'm about to speak a man of around fifty emerges out of nowhere and asks to be served first. I thought he hadn't seen me, a simple and innocent lack of attention. I was wrong. And in a big way. The man looks at me disdainfully and says:

"I was here first. Do you understand Italian?"

"I understand Italian perfectly. You are rude."

"Look at this! A speaking mummy! Why don't you go back to your own country! Why do you come here to make trouble, to spread fanaticism and plant bombs, eh?"

"You're an imbecile."

"Go back to Afghanistan in your burka, or else I'm gonna get really pissed off and give you a beating."

The imbecile gives me a shove, and I lose my balance and fall down. Aida starts crying. I feel a knot in my throat. I can hardly breathe. People gather in a circle around us to enjoy the show entitled "The Veiled Maya and the Racist Idiot." Someone reaches out a hand to help me up. Now I can't keep from crying. I struggle to open my eyes, and I see him: the nameless Arab, the Arab Marcello. He says, "*Ma tkhafish*, don't be afraid." Then he speaks harshly to the imbecile. As long as I've lived in Italy I've never heard an Arab, an immigrant, a foreigner, speak such perfect Italian.

I'm preoccupied with getting Aida away immediately, because she's really scared, and so unfortunately I leave without thanking the Arab Marcello. But in my heart of hearts I hope I'll see him again soon. When I get home I decide not to say anything to my husband. What would be the use? Best to forget about it. I know him too well. He'll use the affair to shut me up in the house or not let me go out by myself anymore. To tell you the truth it's not the first time I've been a victim of racism. I'm sure that my veil is only a pretext. Nuns also wear a sort of veil. Why doesn't anything happen to them? And what about girls who wear miniskirts or go around half naked? They're free and I'm not? That's not right! What happened to all the fine speeches about democracy, individual freedom, and the right to diversity?

Over time I've become united with my veil. Yes, I really have. It's true that I didn't choose it, but now it's the symbol of my identity; rather, it's a second skin. And so? So what. I not only have to accept it; I have to defend it publicly. It's not a question of the veil, the clothing, the fabric, it's a question of dignity. If they don't accept my veil it means that they reject my religion, my culture, my country, my language, my family—in other words, my entire existence. And that is unacceptable.

I make lunch for the architect and Aida. I have no appetite myself. I'm still shaken by what happened at the market. It's not easy to put up with insults. Damn racists, they're just ignorant. That brute thought my veil was a burkha! They are two extremely different things. And then he told me to go and live in Afghanistan! Let him go there, he's nothing but a nasty imbecile. What do I have to do with a burka and Afghanistan?

At four my husband leaves the house to go to work. I get ready to go down to the second floor, to Samira's. Today I have a professional appointment, a new client is waiting, a girl who wants to change her hairstyle. Suddenly the doorbell rings, and I go to open the door.

"*Assalamu aleikum*, sister."

"*Aleikum salam.*"

What a surprise. With no warning, Aisha, alias Signora Haram, has come to see me. She's the wife of the butcher Rami, who pretends to be an imam and is crazy about prohibitions. Paola, that's her real name, is an Italian who converted to Islam ten years ago. She's more or less my age and wears the *niqab*, oh Lord, that complete veil which covers the entire body except the eyes. Her great ambition is to someday bring us the fashion item of the century: the burka on Viale Marconi and environs! Let's hope she never succeeds.

"Sister, I've come to give you some advice."

"You want to lead me back on the right path?"

"Look, consider me an older sister who only wants what's best for you."

"Excuse me, get to the point. I've got an appointment."

"Exactly. I would like to talk to you about your secret work."

"My secret work?"

"I know that you cut hair at Samira's."

"So?"

"It's *haram*, strictly forbidden by Islam."

"Why?"

"We should encourage women to conceal their hair, not display it, to excite men."

"But I cut hair for non-Muslim women."

"You have a duty to convert them to Islam, the only salvation in this world."

"I see. Is there something else?"

"I heard what happened in the market this morning."

"In the market?"

"Yes, the attack of that godless criminal."

"I see you're very well informed."

"Let's say frankly that the reason is your colored veil."

"My veil?"

"In Islam it must be black."

"Really?"

"A colored veil causes confusion and temptation, that is, *fitna*."

"Really? Who says so?"

"There's a fatwa."

"A fatwa against my veil! Issued by whom? By your husband's *halal* butcher shop?"

"I will not allow you to insult my husband. He's a very respectable imam."

"Imam? And where did he study Islam? Maybe at the University of Al Azhar?"

"Don't be funny."

"No, you and your husband stop spreading extremist opinions."

"Us, extremists? We are true Muslims."

"Don't talk nonsense. Don't kid yourself."

"You are a *kafira*, an unbeliever."

"That's enough. Get out of my house."

"You won't get away with this."

She's threatening me! When it comes to Islam, all she knows is *fitna* and fatwa. She accused me of being an unbeliever. But I'm a good Muslim. That's it, I can't stand her, I don't want her around. Enough is enough!

I met Aisha when I arrived in Rome. She invited me to a meeting with other Egyptian and Arab women. The theme of the discussion was the superiority of Islam and the impossibility of living with Christians and Jews. This idea did not convince me, either then or now, because in high school my best friend was a Coptic Christian. That was my first and last meeting at her house. I never went back.

If I remember correctly, she came to see me here at home a couple of times. The first time she wanted to talk to me about the absolute obedience we owe our husbands. Husbands or God? No, husbands! Really. I would say that my grandmother is more liberated than she is. The second time was to collect money for the opening of a new mosque organized by her husband. I have doubts about her mental health. She's like a programmed robot. I think her husband the butcher, playing the imam, has decisively infected her with fanaticism.

I go to Samira's house, trying to forget the face of that stupid Signora Haram. My new client is waiting for me. She's a psychology student who says she got my number from a friend. I'm pleased that the word of mouth system is functioning. I'm working for my professional future. It will all be easier when I open my hairdressing salon for women, inshallah. I've already got the name. Guess what it is: Sofia's Salon.

I like to talk to my clients before I start using the scissors. In my opinion, hair is an important part of character. And this is especially true for women. For instance, a woman who's depressed begins to neglect her hair first of all. Taking care of your hair requires commitment and constancy, it's not something you do from time to time. It has to become a daily habit. It's like having a garden on your head, which has to be tended to every day.

That's it, I'm a sort of gardener, I cut hair very delicately, as if I were cutting flowers. Of course, like all occupations this one has its secrets. To be a hairdresser it's not enough to have scissors and a comb. It's important to observe the face carefully — forehead, eyes, nose, neck—and the rest of the body as well. In other words, you have to look for physical and psychological harmony.

The girl is very pleased with the haircut. She promises not only that she'll return but will do some advertising for me. When she leaves I have tea with Samira. I take the opportunity to tell her the dream about the Trevi fountain. At the end of the story comes my friend's interpretation, punctual and precise.

"Maybe your heart has found its soul mate."

"Which means?"

"That is, you're in love!"

"Come on, Samira, don't make fun of me like the Gypsies who read your palm. I'm a married woman with a child."

"So what? You're a married woman, in love not with your husband but with another man."

"But it's only a dream."

"No, the dream is an inner voice that comes directly from the heart."

According to Samira, I have all the symptoms of love. I don't deny that I like the Arab Marcello. But I'm a married woman with a child. I don't want to act like a teenager. Of course, my married life isn't going well. Just the other day the architect returned to the subject that is so dear to him: having a second child. I don't want to fight. The problem is that

I've run out of arguments against it: life is expensive, let's wait a while, it's not the right moment, I agree but . . . et cetera. The truth is that I don't want to have another child with him. I don't feel like it. That's all. But I have a feeling that this business will not end here. I know my husband, when he gets something into his mind there's no way to make him change it. Let's just hope for the best.

Issa

As I'm about to leave the house Omar the Bangladeshi stops me, saying he wants to talk to me. We sit in the kitchen, across from each other. This time Omar isn't smiling. He looks at me seriously and with some concern.

"Tunisian, you've got to get out right away!"

"Get out? Why?"

"Have you forgotten everything?"

"What have I forgotten?"

"The fight at the market?"

"The fight because of that girl with the veil?"

Of course—Omar works at the market on Viale Marconi, so he was present at the fight with that racist asshole. I had to intervene to stop him. I didn't think twice about helping that beautiful woman in the veil, whom I'd followed from the park in Piazza Meucci. To hell with Judas's precautions! I also discovered then that the little girl isn't her daughter because she called her by her name: Sofia.

That bastard. We nearly came to blows after yelling insults. Anyway, a strange thing happened. While the shit was digging in his pocket for something, maybe a knife, a young man stopped him. I recognized him—it was Antar, my Egyptian "colleague." But what was he doing here on the sidelines? Had he come to shop or was he here for some business having to do with our mission?

Omar is worried about my safety because he knows the other guy well. His nickname says it all: the Beast. He's a neighborhood bully and has a criminal record. "He's a dangerous ex-convict," the Bangladeshi repeats. He says he's sworn to get me at the first opportunity. He already knows all about me: who I am, where I come from, where I work, where I live. In other words, I'd better keep a lookout.

"You see, Tunisian? You've got to leave right away."

"I'm not afraid."

"He's a violent criminal. He's already beaten up a lot of immigrants. You challenged him in public."

"So?"

"He'll get his revenge."

"I don't care."

"It's not worth risking your life, Tunisian."

I've got a little problem. I have to admit I underestimated the situation. Maybe I should talk to Captain Judas about it. Certainly he won't be happy. I went way beyond the job he assigned me. But the positive thing is that I'm becoming the Robin Hood of the poor immigrants of Viale Marconi.

After breakfast, cappuccino and a *cornetto* with jam, I go to Little Cairo. It's the ideal place to meet new people and get information of various types without being noticed. It's like being in a train station or an airport, everyone is worrying about himself and just doesn't have time to bother about his neighbor. In other words, no one is aware of your presence. My cover is effective: I live and work in the neighborhood. But it's pointless to keep talking about cover if I'm not getting results.

I call the family in Tunis, my "mamma" answers. This time we spend the whole time on "papa's" business situation. Business is getting worse and worse, the grocery store isn't doing as well as it used to. He's decided to try something new, because of the unfair and ruthless competition from the supermarkets. The big fish eats the little fish, as the proverb says.

After the phone call I glance at Al Jazeera. There's no big

news, in spite of George W. Bush's wars in Afghanistan and Iraq. People are expecting another one, against Iran, or maybe Syria. Bush the son is a hopeless Texan; as a child he was a fan of Westerns—he was crazy about the phrase "Wanted, Dead or Alive." He wanted to be a sheriff when he grew up; fate granted his wish beyond his rosiest expectations. Instead of being just a sheriff in Texas, he is expanding onto a planetary scale. Can you be happy while the world goes to hell? And what about climate change? And the hole in the ozone layer? Forget about it. I once read an article in a magazine that said that coming generations won't know what snow is. But not to panic, skiing won't disappear: there will be artificial snow. In short, the future promises nothing good? But don't be ridiculous!

I go up to two young Egyptians, one with a big nose and the other with a scar on his forehead. What are they talking about? About the possible amnesty for illegal immigrants. A fixed idea, a real obsession for a lot of people. In these days I've been able study the subject. I can join the discussion with no problems. Here at Little Cairo no one pays attention to formalities, the public debates are open to all—something like the May 1st concert at the church of San Giovanni. Before interrupting I pretend to be listening seriously. The conversation is heating up. Anyway, even I will have some nonsense to say or a position to support. Too bad, though, I'm not in time to open my mouth.

Suddenly a guy with a thick black beard comes in. He's wearing a loose white shirt, and scent. He booms out an *Assalamu aleikum* that reaches the ears of every single person in Little Cairo. Shit, what a voice! He could be a muezzin with no need for a loudspeaker. He's kind of savage-looking, incredible—he's like an actor stepping out of a film set in the time of the Prophet Mohammed. While he stops to chat with Akram, the guy with the big nose turns to me and says in a whisper, "God help us!"

"Who's that?"

"Rami, the butcher. Everyone calls him Signor Haram, but behind his back."

"Why is he called that?"

The guy doesn't answer. He seems afraid. Of whom? And why? What's going on? Problems related to Egyptian solidarity. After a couple of minutes Signor Haram says goodbye to Akram but instead of leaving he turns, comes over to us, and gives me a strong handshake. The guy with the big nose is trembling. Signor Haram asks the guy with the scar about his sick child, then looks at me and says, staring into my eyes,

"Hello, brother, we don't know each other."

"I've only lived on Viale Marconi a short time."

"Welcome! I'm Sheikh Rami."

"My name is Issa, I'm Tunisian."

"There's no difference between Egyptians and Tunisians. We are all brothers in Islam."

I nod, with a timid smile; I prefer not to fuel this conversation. It's better to listen and to answer possible questions very prudently. Signor Haram leaves me alone (for the moment?) and turns his attention to the guy with the big nose—on with the interrogation.

"Brother, I don't see you anymore at the mosque, don't tell me you've given up prayer?"

"No, I always pray."

"So you go to another mosque?"

"No, I pray at home."

"Ah, you pray at home. And why?"

"I don't have time to go to the mosque."

"You don't have time to devote to Almighty God, eh?"

"No, I don't mean that."

"May God forgive you."

" . . . "

"Are you still working as a pizza maker?"

"Yes."

"In the same Italian restaurant?"

"Yes."

"I've told you repeatedly that that work is *haram*. Why do you persist on the path of sin, eh?"

"I'm a good Muslim. I recite the prayers every day."

"That's not enough. Do you make pizza with prosciutto, yes or no?"

"Yes, but I don't eat pork and I've never taken a drop of wine."

"Don't say 'but.' Touching pork is *haram*. This is not a personal opinion; it's a fatwa from our great teachers."

"But it's the only work I know how to do. If I leave it I could end up unemployed."

"Brother, you should have more faith in God. If you are obedient and follow his rules he will never abandon you. God Almighty says in the Koran that he will provide for all of his creatures."

The kid with the big nose doesn't respond, he seems resigned to defeat. Signor Haram continues his sermon, quoting verses from the Koran and repeatedly citing the example of the Prophet. He's very excited, he seems utterly convinced that he's right, or, rather, that he possesses the absolute truth. At some point he remembers my presence.

"And what mosque do you pray in?"

"None."

"So you, too, pray at home?"

"No, I don't pray."

"What? Aren't you a Muslim?"

"I'm a Muslim, but I'm not observant."

"That's very serious, brother. May God lead you on the right path!"

"Amen."

"What kind of work do you do?"

"I'm a dishwasher."

"Where?"

"In an Italian restaurant."

"Then my earlier discussion goes for you, too, brother."

How wonderful! He devotes five generous minutes to explaining to me that my job as a dishwasher is *haram*. The reason? Always the same. Touching pork and alcoholic beverages is an impure act. As a result, the money I earn, even cleaning the toilets, is like stolen money or drug money.

Before he leaves us, Signor Haram shakes our hands again, harder than before. He wants to leave his mark, not with words alone. Watching him go, I wonder if this is all just a joke. But unfortunately no, Signor Haram has spoken the truth. The fatwa prohibiting Muslim immigrants from working in restaurants is a real disaster. What will happen to the pizza makers, cooks, dishwashers (like me), barmen, and waiters? The overwhelming majority of Egyptians in Italy work in restaurants. What a mess!

In the afternoon I go to work. I arrive at the restaurant punctually, Damiano is already off to a flying start with the whiskey. I think he's an alcoholic, but he doesn't realize it. Luckily he has a strong body and he holds his liquor. But till when? Who knows. Felice is making the dough for the pizza.

"Issa, we have a big problem."

"Are you talking about the fatwa?"

"What fatwa?"

"The one against working in restaurants."

"Are you referring to Signor Haram?"

Felice is informed about everything. He doesn't hide his hostility toward the Egyptian butcher. He tells me a few things about him. It seems that the fatwa against working in restaurants isn't the first and certainly won't be the last. Signor Haram doesn't have any troubles with his residency permit. Lucky him! He became a citizen because he's married to an

Italian. So he has plenty of time to spend on his bullshit. He seems to have a taste for terrorizing poor Muslim immigrants, especially Egyptians, with extremist judgments: forbidding them to watch TV, listen to music, shake hands with members of the opposite sex, live with non-Muslims, touch a dog, go to a doctor who is not of the same sex, have a bank account, take out a loan, etc.

In other words, he sees prohibitions everywhere. He earned his nickname by coming up with a new prohibition every damn day. Instead of doing a good job as a butcher, he devotes himself to spreading oddball religious opinions. Someone like him, with his extraordinary expertise, should live not in Rome but in some Afghan village taken over by the Taliban.

His greatest ambition is to become imam of the big mosque in Rome, even though he hasn't studied at Al Azhar, which is the usual requirement. Who knows, sooner or later he'll end up on Bruno Vespa's talk show. And you won't want to miss it!

Felice tells me a tragicomic story involving Imam Rami alias Signor Haram and his adversary, Imam Zaki alias Signor Halal:

Saturday is a bad day for pizza makers. You work like a dog. Felice quarrels with a waiter for a silly reason and in a moment of rage declares, "I swear by God I'll divorce my wife if they don't get rid of this bastard of a waiter." After closing, Felice asks Damiano to fire the waiter, presenting his version of events. The boss tries to mediate, asking the guy to take a step back and apologize to Felice, who, in turn, tries to explain that it's a matter of the oath and divorce: "If this waiter doesn't leave, I can't go to bed with my wife." The waiter keeps asking the same question: "What do I have to do with your wife?" Felice doesn't answer. In other words, apologies are not enough to save the marriage.

In the end Damiano refuses his request. "I don't want to throw somebody out in the street just to satisfy a Muslim religious whim." Felice now finds himself in a very awkward situation. He decides to go to Signor Haram to get a religious opinion, and Signor Haram, naturally, has no doubts: the oath sanctions the divorce. In desperation, Felice also consults Signor Halal, who gives a completely different opinion: there is no divorce, because his wife has nothing to do with it. Felice takes the second position and the matter is closed.

"But Issa, let's forget Signor Haram and his fatwas. I wanted to speak to you about something else."

"What?"

"Farid, the assistant pizza maker, leaves tomorrow for Egypt and he'll be there for three months—it seems that his father is dying. He's afraid he'll lose his job when he returns. Will you substitute for him in the meantime?"

"But I've never done it."

"Don't worry, I'll teach you everything. You don't want to be a dishwasher your whole life?"

"No, no . . . All right, I'll do it. Thank you. When do I start?"

"Right away. I'll talk to Damiano."

That same night I replace the Egyptian assistant pizza maker, while a Pakistani fellow takes my place as dishwasher. Felice explains the secrets of the work skillfully and patiently, dwelling on the fact that for many years he was the assistant to a Neapolitan pizza maker. In other words, he learned from a true professional.

The dough is very important. The recipe has to remain secret, like the recipe for Coca-Cola. Every pizza maker has his personal dough. Later, but only later, he can indulge his imagination and make up new pizzas by mixing different ingredients. Felice considers himself an architect of pizza. He has a list of pizzas that he has created, like Nile pizza, Zamalek (his favorite team), Aida (the name of his daughter), and so on.

During the brief pauses between one pizza and the next

Felice talks to me in particular about Farid. He's really angry at him. You can't leave like that, without any warning and for that length of time. Plus he expects to find his job waiting when he gets back. It seems that the assistant pizza maker has invented yet another lie with the story of his father's illness. The real reason for the trip to Egypt is to go and have a good time with his wife, left with her parents in Cairo.

"You understand, Issa? Farid couldn't stand abstinence."

"Abstinence?"

"Yes, he was in need of sexual assistance. He went to fuck. Hahaha."

Felice tells me a lot of details about the lives of Muslim immigrants, especially the observant ones. Many of them live in profound anxiety. The married ones, for instance, can't return home every year. And they can't have extramarital relations, because Islam forbids it. Bachelors, for their part, are also forced to be celibate, in expectation of marrying. And in the meantime they have to confront all the problems associated with sexuality, like premature ejaculation or even impotence. Felice also remarks on the Italian girls and foreign tourists who go around half naked, exciting the these wretched Muslim immigrants.

My first night as an assistant pizza maker went very well. Felice told me that I learned quickly. But I don't go home with him, Damiano asks me to give the new dishwasher a hand cleaning up. Finally after another twenty minutes I'm heading home. All of a sudden a car shoots full speed out of Via Oderisi da Gubbio and stops a hairsbreadth away from me. Bastard! He almost hit me! Immediately I think of the Beast in the market on Viale Marconi and his promise of revenge. Should I run or challenge him? There he is, sticking his head out the window. But no, it's not him.

"Get in!"

"Fuck! Are you trying to kill me?"

"I told you to get in!"

That shit Captain Judas! What happened? Why has he abandoned the usual precautions? We shouldn't ever be seen here. Our next appointment was set for tomorrow morning in Via Nazionale. He's going to blow my cover like this.

"I see you're scared."

"Fucking shit, you were about to hit me!"

"Truthfully, were you afraid of the Beast?"

"The Beast? I see that your colleague Antar has spread the story."

"I was told that at the market you spoke perfect Italian. Bravo, congratulations."

"I made a mistake."

"You risked messing up your cover."

"It won't happen again."

"The girl with the veil, do you know her?"

"No."

"Sure?"

"I swear."

"Anyway you don't have to worry about the Beast. We've taken him out of your way. It wasn't hard to arrest him for dealing. At this very hour he is sleeping in the Regina Coeli prison."

"You wanted to tell me that?"

"No, I came to give you some other remarkable news."

"Please."

"You remember the information about the explosives?"

"Yes."

"We've received confirmation that the Goma-2 Eco is here in Viale Marconi."

"Really?"

"You'd better get a move on, Tunisian."

"What should I do?"

"You're acting like a boy scout on a camping trip!"

"I'm doing everything possible."

"So far you haven't found out a goddamn thing!"

"I can't perform miracles—my name is Christian, not Christ."

"You'll make me look like shit with my superiors, not to mention my American and Egyptian colleagues."

"I don't give a fuck about your colleagues. I'm sick and tired of this business."

"You can't walk out of it now, understand?"

I can't find words to describe the reaction of this fucking Captain Judas. Whenever he decides to break my balls he succeeds wonderfully. I listen unwillingly to his preaching. The usual warmed-over crap. Finally he lets me out, at the Marconi bridge. I go home feeling destroyed and with my morale in the pits. I don't have the slightest desire to sleep—maybe I'm afraid I'll have nightmares. Damn terrorists, where have you hidden the explosives? When and where will you unleash the inferno?

SOFIA

I close the bedroom door so I can listen to the radio without disturbing my architect while I get through the housework, even if it's not that easy to wake him. He's a really heavy sleeper. You'd need a band with trumpets around his bed to wake him up. Luckily he doesn't snore. It's not a small consideration. Giulia told me that there are couples who split up just because of it. And so? So what. I would say that in Italy people divorce for rather trivial reasons, or am I wrong?

I'm listening to a really interesting program on one of the RAI radio channels. It's a discussion of domestic violence against women. It's incredible: women are subjected to psychological, physical, and sexual violence not only on the street, coming home from work at night, or in underground parking garages but also, in fact especially, at home. Yes, at home. Who would have guessed? The guilty parties are called husbands, companions, fiancés, fathers, brothers, or sons. The guests on the program are mainly women who are involved in this issue.

But what's striking to me is the statistics presented by the host: "In Italy more than six and a half million women have suffered, at least once in their life, some form of physical or sexual violence. More than sixty percent of such women are mistreated by their partner or a person they know, and more than ninety-five percent do not report the violence they suffer, probably out of fear of the consequences."

To tell the truth, this radio discussion of domestic violence really stuns me. Why? I thought women were victims of violence in war zones, like Afghanistan or Iraq, or in countries where there's racism, like some African Muslim countries, and where poverty and ignorance are widespread. But not in Italy! In other words, isn't Italy still a European country, Western, part of the G-8, and so on, or am I wrong?

Around ten I go with Aida to the park in Piazza Meucci to take advantage of the sunny morning. There is no sign of my two friends—they're not coming today. Yesterday I talked on the phone to Dorina, and she told me that Grandfather Giovanni isn't feeling well, so he'll read *La Padania, Libero,* and *Il Giornale* sitting comfortably in his living room, at least for now. Giulia, meanwhile, has an appointment with the pediatrician, because her son has stomachaches that won't go away.

I watch my daughter playing with two little girls. She's calm and serene. I'm sure that her childhood will be different from mine and my sisters'. I don't know if she'll be happy. Only God Almighty knows. Everything will depend on her *maktùb.* Yet I'm sure about one thing: she won't suffer the absolutely worst kind of domestic violence, which is female circumcision. This is not a promise but an oath that I intend to keep at all costs. My little darling, your mamma will never let anyone hurt you!

Ah, the wounds of memory don't heal with time. Where should I begin my story about the circumcision of girls? Good question!

Maybe before elementary school. In our neighborhood there was a toothless old hag who seemed like the incarnation of the wicked witch in the fairy tales. She was a specialist in the matter, and indescribably cruel. I've never hated anyone as much as her. Now she's dead and I hope from the depths of my soul that she ended up in Hell forever. In Arabic they say, "*La tajuz ala al-mayyit illa arrahma,*" pity the dead. I'm not usually a resentful person. But that was too much!

My sister Nadia, the oldest, was the first to be subjected to this torture. I don't like to say things in a roundabout way.

Samira taught me an Algerian proverb about hypocrisy: "Come out naked and God will dress you." It would be impossible to describe her psychological and physical pain. The pain lasted a long time and perhaps will continue for her whole life.

Then it was my sister Zeineb's turn—she's a year older than me. In her case, too, it's reasonable to speak of torture, inflicted, what's more, on a child of seven years old. It's a true crime against humanity, worse than rape, because the instigators are the parents! And so? So what. I think the parents have a tremendous responsibility. Would female circumcision exist without the consent of the family? Zeineb almost died, because of a hemorrhage and then a serious infection. Luckily she was taken to the hospital right away, and the doctors performed a true miracle to save her. That evil toothless witch was not a doctor but a complete illiterate, so it didn't even minimally cross her mind that she should disinfect the scissors, her tool for the job—or, rather, the weapon of the crime.

Zeineb remains traumatized. There is no hope of healing or of forgetting. The circumcised woman is a kind of invisible handicapped person, unrecognized. She doesn't even have the right to complain, or to mourn her fate. In fact, she's supposed to thank everyone who had a part in her circumcision for preserving her purity and protecting her reputation! The truth is that men fear the sexual power of women and the idea is to eliminate it through castration. To hell with purity and reputation. I know that I am a Muslim with a veil and am not supposed to curse (that's for men only, at least among us that's the case). I allow myself to say just one, though not in Arabic, so as not to feel uneasy: "Fuck you!" God forgive me.

The experience has conditioned Zeineb's life. She got married five years ago, and had a child only after many difficulties. She always says to me: "I'm fifty percent woman." She can't have a normal sex life. Her husband is a good man, he says he loves her and won't ever leave her. Is it true? Only God knows.

Truthfully, I don't believe in eternal love, it's the stuff of soap operas—Egyptian, Brazilian, Mexican, Turkish.

"Do you love me?"

"Yes."

"How much do you love me?"

"Very much."

"When do you love me?"

"I love you in spring, I love you in summer, I love you in fall, and I love you in winter. I love you always."

"My love, light of my eyes, sun of my days. I'll love you forever."

"I love you more than I love myself."

"Our love is as pure and abundant as our mothers' milk."

"My love! Let's live our love until death do us part."

Words, words, words, as that Italian song says. Reality is one thing, fiction another. Unfortunately my sister is not a character in a soap opera. So far her marriage is solid, but it could crumble at any moment. Life is never predictable. The truth is that she lives in terror of being abandoned, rejected, replaced by another woman: by a hundred-percent woman.

Men are a rather complicated breed, which in my opinion hasn't been sufficiently studied. People often speak of female moods. And what about male moods? Men whose attitude can change from one moment to the next. Today they say, "You're the woman of my life." Then they come back the next day and tell you, "I'm sorry, I'm going to live with another woman. Bye." Is that normal behavior?

For my sister Zeineb circumcision marked the beginning of a nightmare. And obviously an early end to childhood.

When my turn came the situation had changed somewhat. Lucky for me. What happened? Was the circumcision of girls abolished in Egypt? Were those who actually performed the operation arrested and punished? Were the instigators—that is, our beloved parents—put on trial? No, nothing of the sort. Something simple happened, something quite banal. After the tragedy of my sister the family decided not to go to the horrible toothless witch. Looking for a replacement took some time.

My aunt Amina (my father's sister, not to mention my guardian angel) had an ingenious idea. She suggested taking me to a friend of hers, a nurse who performed female circumcision. I trusted my aunt blindly and I knew that she wouldn't let anyone hurt me. And in fact the nurse friend didn't exist.

We went to Aunt Amina's house to carry out the plan. First: no one touched my clitoris. Second: she stained my underpants with the blood of a hen that had just been killed. Third: I was to make an effort to cry. A river of tears. The success of the plan depended on my bravura performance. I gave it my best. Everything went smoothly. The next day, my mother discovered the trick, but she didn't have the courage to expose it. She couldn't, after the tragedy of my sister. My father and the rest of the family remained in the dark. For a few months my mother, my aunt, and I shared the secret. Then other people found out, all women obviously. Men prefer to stay out of it, this is women's business and should remain among women, like menstruation.

Was I very fortunate? Certainly. But it wasn't just plain sailing. I went through childhood and adolescence afraid of being found out and having to suffer the same fate as my sisters. I had terrifying nightmares with the toothless old hag as the main character. Not to mention the sense of guilt of the privileged. Why was I saved and not my sisters?

I still remember the celebration when my brother Imad was circumcised. It was a really grand occasion. I often wondered: why is circumcision for males a celebration while for females it's like a funeral, or anyway done in secret? And also: they say that female circumcision is an Islamic tradition, but I can't find any trace of it in the Koran. Its supporters cite a *hadith* of our

Prophet in which He doesn't clearly forbid the practice, but, as everyone knows, not all the quotations are authentic.

Recently the religious authorities at Al Azhar University woke up. (Better late than never.) They stated that female circumcision is not a religious obligation, and that, in fact, it's harmful to women's health. So if that's the case, why don't they ban it immediately, as they did rape and drugs? Damn the devil! All they have to say is, "The circumcision of girls is *haram*." Some time ago I heard on the radio that the Italian parliament is drafting a law against female circumcision, which is still practiced in some immigrant communities in Italy. I'm in favor. It's a further protection for girls like my daughter.

Samira comes from Algeria, and in the Maghreb female circumcision doesn't exist. Why are the majority of Egyptian girls circumcised? Why is it so prevalent in Egypt (even among Coptic Christians), in Sudan, and in the countries of the Gulf, but not anywhere else? This proves that female circumcision is not a religious obligation like prayer and Ramadan.

Maybe it's more correct to speak of genital mutilation? Women who suffer the torture of female circumcision should be considered victims of war. I think female circumcision is like rape. There's no difference. I have no doubts about this. What sense does it make to exchange traditions that should be respected for customs that are disastrous and dangerous to the religion itself? Of course we can always say that Islam has nothing to do with it. But what can we say about Muslims? Are they responsible or not? Are the parents of girls innocent or complicit?

Two years ago I saw a really good documentary on TV. It was about a French surgeon who specializes in the reconstruction of the clitoris. This is not cosmetic surgery. Many, many women, victims of the worst domestic violence, go to this surgeon to regain their dignity. It's a simple operation, and there's no danger to the woman's health.

It would be fantastic if my sister Zeineb could have the operation. A wonderful dream that would put an end to the nightmare of the toothless witch. The operation is expensive. For my part, I'm doing all I can to help her, by saving some money. So I continue to cut hair secretly in Samira's apartment. The architect knows nothing about it. I hide the money behind the couch in the living room. I can't open an account in a bank or the post office.

A few weeks ago I saw the film *La Ciociara,* with Sophia Loren, for the third time. It takes place during the Second World War, and it's very sad. Loren plays a young mother who flees Rome with her daughter because of the bombing. The two take refuge in the countryside. At the end of the movie they're raped in an abandoned bombed-out church by a bunch of soldiers in turbans. Giulia told me that they were Moroccans. This scene makes me cry, because I identify, every time, with both the mother and the daughter.

Being in the park without the company of Dorina and Giulia is not the greatest. A woman in a veil sitting by herself on a public bench does not go unnoticed. I prefer to avoid the problem, so I leave.

I go to the Marconi library. Maybe I'll find a movie in VHS to borrow. There aren't many people here today. I take the opportunity to glance at the papers. What a surprise! What a pleasant surprise! From a distance I see the Arab Marcello, sitting near the window, reading a magazine. I can't pretend I don't see him. I have to say hello.

"Hello."

"Hello."

"I wanted to thank you for what you did the other day at the market."

"I didn't do anything. It's a duty."

"Sadly there's always a rotten apple among the good ones."

"Right. No need to generalize."

"Not all Italians are ignorant or racist."

"Luckily."

"I don't want to disturb you."

"You're not disturbing me at all."

"I'll let you read. Thanks again."

"Not at all."

"Bye."

"Bye."

Why do I turn red? Damn! I forgot to ask him his name. But that's not really a problem. He already has a name: the Arab Marcello. Where is he from? From his accent he doesn't seem Egyptian, or Palestinian, or Lebanese, or Syrian, or Iraqi. I must say that he speaks like Samira. It's true. And so? So what. He must be Algerian. I could solve the puzzle of his native country if I had a recording of his voice to submit to my best friend for examination. Samira always says: "I can tell if someone is Algerian with no problem at all, a word or a glance is enough." I must absolutely arrange for her to see him. The sixth sense exists. And also feminine intuition, we might add. May I say that we women don't miss anything, or am I wrong?

At lunch my architect tries to draw me into a dangerous discussion that is on the verge of turning into an argument. But I really don't feel like arguing.

"You know Akram's wife is pregnant?"

"Really?"

"Yes, Akram will be a father for the fourth time. Lucky him."

"*Mabruk*, congratulations."

"We, on the other hand, can't give Aida a little brother."

"It's *maktùb*."

"*Maktùb* has nothing to do with it. God has given us health. We're healthy."

"Thank God."

"It's you who don't want to."

"I'm sorry, it's not the moment to talk about this. I've had a terrible headache since this morning. I'm going to take an aspirin and lie down for a while."

Usually I don't use the feminine ruse of the headache to avoid some "conjugal obligation." But in this situation I can't do anything else. I have no alternatives. I'm sorry, this time I'm not going to fall for it like a fly in the honey jar.

Have another child now? He absolutely shouldn't talk about it. Akram can be a father for the fourth time or the fortieth, I don't give a damn about him. God alone knows how many children that secret polygamist has brought into the world.

Around six I take Aida and go to Samira's. As soon as she sees me she cries, "Sofia, I have a surprise for you!"

"Really?"

"Yes, I've managed to record the play with Adel Imam."

"Which one?"

"*Sayed the Servant.*"

Fantastic! It's a comedy from the late eighties or early nineties, very famous in the Arab world. What's it about? Well, it tells the story of Sayed, a young servant in a wealthy family. His life is turned upside down after the daughter of the house is divorced for the third time. In exchange for a sum of money, Sayed receives a proposal to be the *muhàllil*, that is, to marry the girl and then divorce her, so that she'll be able to return to her first husband. What? I've already explained the business of divorce in Islam. O.K., I'll repeat it, but this is the last time. Couples are allowed two divorces; after the third no reconciliation is possible. If a couple wants to go back to being husband and wife she has to marry another man, strictly Muslim, consummate the marriage, and then divorce him. Is it clear now?

Back to Sayed, the servant. After he marries the rich girl, things get complicated, because Sayed refuses to divorce her.

The two fall in love. The actor Adel Imam is extraordinary. You could die laughing.

I go home and watch the wonderful *Divorce Italian Style,* with Marcello Mastroianni. The story is entertaining. A Sicilian baron sets up the perfect plot to get rid of his wife and marry another, younger woman, and then . . .

ISSA

I wake up around eight. I don't feel like getting in line for the bathroom. I'm thinking about going to wash my face in the kitchen sink and then heading out to the café to pee in the bathroom there. What to do? The truth is that I feel kind of down, so I decide to lie in bed for a few minutes. In a hurry I'm not. I start thinking about the mission, this damn Little Cairo operation. So far I've gotten no concrete results. It's not easy to flush out professional terrorists who are ready for anything, even death. I dodge the disagreeable question: where is the Goma-2 Eco hidden?

Saber rushes into the room. He's just had a shower, a serious undertaking in this shitty house. He is all sweet-smelling. Lucky him. He's fit and, as usual, in a good mood. Does he have a date with Simona Barberini? Anything is possible. He stares at me and says with a mischievous smile:

"You know who's coming on to me?"

"Simona Barberini?"

"I wish!"

"Who?"

"You won't believe me."

"Come on."

"Teresa, the landlady."

"Teresa!"

"Yes. She wants me to go to bed with her."

"Really?"

"Issa, brebare yourself. Next time will be your turn."

"I can't wait."

Saber tells me a few things about Teresa alias Vacation. It seems that she has a weakness for young Arabs, and this would explain her frequent trips to the Middle East and North Africa. I don't think Saber is a liar who invents stuff out of whole cloth. Probably he's telling the truth. His theory is convincing.

"You know why Teresa rents the house to us?"

"To make money."

"No. She's rich. There's another reason."

"What is it?"

"Teresa uses the abartment to attract new studs. You get it now?"

Saber tries to lend support to his argument by citing the cases of many young Arabs seduced by Signora Teresa. If you agree to play the game you can have a lot of benefits, like, for example, not paying rent. Saber has already refused an invitation to dinner, which is the first step to ending up in her bed.

"Issa, you remember Teresa's sby?"

"Yes."

"Now we have brove."

"Who is it?"

"Omar, the Bangladeshi."

"Really?"

"Yes, really. The Bangladeshi always live among themselves. Why did he come to live with us?"

On the way out I see Ibrahima sitting in the kitchen by himself, staring at the ceiling. Strange, what's he doing here at this hour? Usually he goes out early in the morning to sell his counterfeit purses. I greet him and sit down across from him. The Senegalese has a sad, weary expression and he avoids looking me in the eyes. He doesn't seem to feel like joking.

"You look kind of down, Ibrahima."

"I've got some problems, brother."

"Family?"

"No, work, even if according to the law I don't work, I'm still a smuggler and a fence. To them I'm a criminal."

"But what happened?"

"The cops are bastards—they gave me another fine and confiscated all my merchandise, damn it."

Ibrahim explains to me briefly his difficult situation. He's not worried about the fine, because over the years he's collected a lot of fines and has never paid one. The real problem is the confiscation of the merchandise. Now he has no capital and can't buy new merchandise. The wholesalers aren't generous and understanding the way they used to be. Today most of them are Chinese and they won't accept a promise to pay, they want the money immediately. Ibrahima is worried not so much for himself as for the support of his family in Senegal.

"Brother, it's hard to be the father of a family. Every month I have to send two hundred euros."

"How will you manage now?"

"I don't know. Worse than the fine and the loss of the merchandise, one of the cops insulted me, a cop *con la facia da cul de can da cacia*—with a face like a hound's ass, as they say in Milan."

"What did he say to you?"

"He called me a filthy shit black bastard son of slaves."

"Dirty racist bastard!"

"Brother, in Italy there's racism among the Italians themselves. In Milan they say 'Hey, southerner. Go back where you came from.' In other words, fuck off."

Yesterday "Hey, southerner," today "Hey, non-European, Moroccan, black." What should we do? It sort of makes me laugh to hear the Senegalese speaking the Milanese dialect. I know that Captain Judas will not be very happy about my initiative. He'll tell me I'm acting like a social worker or a volunteer for some charity, but I don't give a shit. I've decided to give Ibrahima two hundred euros. At first he won't accept it—we all have our money problems, he says, it's not right. But I insist until I persuade him. We agree on the fact that it's a loan (without interest and to be repaid as soon as possible). Ibrahima gives me a warm embrace.

I go to the bar with a double objective: to pee and to get breakfast. In the end I give up the *cornetto* and am satisfied with an espresso to cheer myself up. I realize I've gotten very thin. I don't have to rack my brains to discover the reason. I'm stressed. It certainly would be better not to let my real mother see me. I'm practically unrecognizable.

After the coffee I go over to Little Cairo. I call the "family" in Tunisia. A male voice answers: "It's your father." My Tunisian "papa"! What a surprise. It's the first time I've spoken to him. The phone call goes without complications for two reasons. One, a good Arab son shouldn't talk to his father but listen. It's a sign of respect. Second, I know about his business troubles, so I confine myself to asking for news. My "father" is very succinct, not like the "mamma." Five minutes is enough for him to summarize the matter. Now he's found a tiny opening, a way of getting out of the crisis: transform the grocery store into a call center. You have to keep up with the changes in society. Before the final goodbye he gives me a series of instructions: don't drink alcoholic beverages, don't spend time with criminals, don't get into debt, etc. Nothing about women. It's a delicate subject. Arab fathers are old-fashioned, it's not easy for them to talk to their sons about women and, especially, sex.

After the phone call, I'm kind of at loose ends, so I settle in to watch TV. It's always the same channel, Al Jazeera. There's a repeat of a program about women. I sit glued to the screen, because the subject is interesting: sexual molestation in the Arab world. It's the first time in my life that I've heard Muslim women speak openly about sexuality on television. It's a real cultural revolution. A couple of years ago in Tunis I met a graduate student from Oxford who was doing a thesis on Al Jazeera. According to him a democratization is taking place in the Arab countries, thanks to the satellite channels. The autocratic regimes are no longer able to exercise censorship. People are beginning to speak more freely on three taboo subjects: sex, politics, and religion. Too bad, the program's over, I got here too late.

Coming out of Little Cairo I run into Felice. He's with four people I don't know. They seem to be holding a small public meeting.

"*Assalamu aleikum.*"

"*Aleikum salam*, Issa. We're talking about something of interest to you. Let me introduce brother Zaki, the imam of the Mosque of Peace. We're discussing the fatwa against working in Italian restaurants."

Here's the imam they've talked about so much. And always in positive terms. His nickname, Signor Halal, was probably given to him to contrast with that of the butcher, Imam Rami alias Signor Haram. He's around forty, well dressed, without the loose shirt or the beard. He has chosen to speak in a simple, clear Italian, not Arabic. It takes me a few minutes to understand the reason: among the listeners is a convert who doesn't know Arabic; his name is Alessandro, but he's called Ali.

Signor Halal has a calm way of speaking; he never raises his voice. He is able to take apart Signor Haram's fatwa point by point, asserting the principle under which the context should take precedence over the text. The Koran has to be interpreted on the basis of the reality we live in. It's damaging to import fatwas from the outside. He notes several times that there is more religious freedom in Italy than in many Muslim countries.

It really seems that Signor Haram's shock fatwa is foundering. Signor Halal is quoting the Prophet when he says, "Facilitate, don't complicate." So the ultimate message is clear:

Muslims are allowed to work in Italian and other Western restaurants.

Before I go to work I stop at Via Nazionale to see Captain Judas. He hasn't arrived yet and I take advantage of that to have a shower. Then I go online and glance at my email. Seventy-nine unread messages. More than half are from Marta. Shit, better to call her right away. This time, too, I use a prepaid card.

"Hi Marta, it's Christian."

"Christian! Where have you been? Why haven't you answered my emails?"

"I'm sorry, I've had a lot to do."

"What are you doing?"

"I'll tell you all about it later."

"When are you coming back?"

"I don't know."

"Give me your number in Tunis."

"I can't."

"Why?"

"I'll explain everything, but not now."

"Christian, where are you calling from?"

"From Tunis."

"Don't lie."

"I'm telling the truth."

"Are you leaving me, Christian?"

"Don't be silly."

"Is there someone else, Christian? Tell me the truth. I have the right to know."

"What are you talking about? There's no other woman, Marta. You're the only one for me."

"You bastard, Christian!"

There, Marta's tantrum arrives right on schedule. It takes me a while to calm her down. I promise to call her more often. I hope to keep my word, otherwise it's going to end badly. I make a rapid series of calls to say hello to my real family, the one that lives in Mazara del Vallo. Everything's O.K. Everyone's fine. No news, good news!

The girl with the veil comes to mind—I don't know why. Last time she had a CD of Om Kalthoum's, and since I've got a good memory, I remember what the title song was: *Awedt Einy*, "I'm Used to Seeing You." I look for it on the Arabic music sites and find it easily. I put on the headphones and listen to the song.

> My eyes are used to seeing you
> My heart has delivered my will to you
> I feel happy when you look at me
> And when you're beside me
> And if a day passes without seeing you
> It doesn't count in the days of my life.

Finally Captain Judas arrives. I'm astonished to see that he's smiling. If there's anything that truly drives me crazy it's men who are moody, like women—now they're happy, now sad, now affectionate and now sullen, now calm and now agitated. At least with women there's some warning—you can be prepared in advance to absorb the blows. I sit down and wait for Captain Judas's pearls of wisdom.

"Dear Tunisian, I've got some good news for you."

"I'm all ears."

"We've discovered the head of the second cell."

"Really? Who is it?"

"He lives in Viale Marconi and he's an imam.'

"Signor Haram!"

"No, the dog that barks doesn't bite."

"Who the hell is it, then?"

"The other one, Imam Zaki, known as Signor Halal."

"You're sure?"

"Of course. You seem bewildered."

"To me he seems like a regular guy. I just met him today."

"Tunisian, appearances are deceiving. These people are skilled in the practice of Taqiyya."

"Taqiyya?"

"You know what it is?"

Of course I know. It's a doctrine followed by certain Shiite sects that exhorts its adherents to hide their beliefs in order to avoid being persecuted. Luckily the courses in Islamic studies I took at the University of Palermo were good for something. It's a shitty doctrine. Should we be suspicious of everyone? Judge intention rather than facts? And how the fuck do you know? I don't have the slightest idea. Judas is convinced that now it will be easier to discover the other members of the cell: we have to look in the entourage of Imam Zaki. So it's likely that Felice is one of them. It would be quite a joke on me: to work with him, see him every day, and not realize anything.

"You'll have to infiltrate the Mosque of Peace."

"How?"

"By going there to pray."

"Me? Are you joking?"

"No, I'm serious."

"It's a delicate thing, I'd like to think about it a little."

"Maybe you don't understand. I'm not asking you to convert to Islam."

"I understand perfectly."

"We're playing the last round. We have to get busy before it's too late, agreed?"

"All right. When should I start?"

"Right away."

"Right away?"

"Yes. Listen . . . one last thing."

"What."

"I would advise you, when you perform the ablutions, don't show your dick. Remember, you're not circumcised, hahaha."

He's laughing, the bastard, he's always ready with a wise-crack. Anyway, I thank him for the valuable advice. All I need is prayer to become a real Muslim! I wanted the bicycle and now I have to pedal.

But why should I complain? This is a real opportunity—a unique experience that would enrich my résumé as an Orientalist, or, rather, an Arabist, as they say in the academic world. I've always distrusted those Westerners who live in Arab countries for years without making the least effort to learn Arabic, and who remain tourists forever, hateful, superficial and spoiled—unbearable. They think they know the country they live in, but really they don't know shit.

After a few minutes Antar alias Starsky and James alias Hutch join us. They are smiling happily, like two children on Christmas. The atmosphere is very cheerful. James has brought a bottle of champagne. He's like a drunk English soccer fan coming out of a pub. He sits down and starts his speech American style. "They called a little while ago from Langley to congratulate me. The discovery of the second cell on Viale Marconi is a tremendous result. We have to organize a big event to disclose the behind-the-scenes details of Operation Little Cairo. We need a press conference with a minister, the Interior or Foreign Minister. Our ambassador in Rome has agreed to participate. Little Cairo should send a clear message to the world: the fight against Islamic terrorism, the war on Terror, as President Bush says, requires international coopera-tion. Let's drink a toast!"

Now it's Antar's turn for a speech, in the Egyptian style, obviously. "I, too, have received congratulations from my supe-riors in Cairo. It's very important to make it clear that our gov-ernment is always in the lead in the fight against terrorism. This war is not against Islam but against terrorists, wherever they are hiding out. Our Minister of the Interior is ready to come to Rome to take part in the celebration."

Judas tries to rein in the enthusiasm and excitement of his colleagues. "It's too soon to think about a press conference—Operation Little Cairo is not over yet. There are in fact two important questions still open. First: where are they hiding the explosives? Second: who is the suicide candidate?

The atmosphere degenerates when James has the idea of seizing Imam Zaki. Antar immediately reminds him of the case of the imam Abu Omar. In response, the C.I.A. agent accuses his Egyptian colleague of amateurism. "You didn't honor the agreement. Abu Omar was supposed to disappear." Antar won't go along and turns the charges against the accuser. "You are the amateurs! You were caught like chickens—you left traces everywhere. And then what were we supposed to do with Abu Omar? Kill him? You Americans are really unbearable. You accuse us of not respecting human rights, then you want us to behave like General Pinochet!"

The Abu Omar case. The scandal that caused a crisis in the relations between Italy and the United States. Judas had already told me about it. The case can be summarized as follows: in February, 2003, a team of C.I.A. agents in Milan seizes, in broad daylight, the imam Abu Omar. He's a forty-year-old Egyptian who has lived in Italy since 1999, after gaining political-refugee status. He is suspected of having ties to international terrorists because of his militancy in the Egyptian organization Gamaa Islamiya and his participation in the war in the former Yugoslavia on the side of the Bosnian Muslims.

Abu Omar is immediately brought to the American military base in Aviano, where he is subjected to torture and various interrogations. The next day he is put on a secret flight and transferred to Egypt, to the terrible prison of Tora, where he spends fourteen months and endures more torture.

His wife reports his disappearance to the Italian police, but there is no trace of him. Finally, in April of 2004, the Egyptian authorities release him, and Abu Omar shows up with his wife and some friends from Milan. The Italian judges, who had begun to intercept his phone calls, start investigating, and the scandal explodes: the Abu Omar case.

Last month the prosecutor in Milan ended the investigation into the kidnapping by charging the C.I.A. agents with violating the sovereignty of the Italian state. But questions remain: did our secret services know? And how was it possible for a political refugee to be handed over to his original country? Instinctively I think of Giuseppe Garibaldi and the hundreds of Mazzinian political opponents in Tunisia, who enjoyed the protection of the Bey of Tunis. No one ever thought of giving them up to Savoy. It should be remembered that a death sentence was hanging over Garibaldi.

Finally Captain Judas manages to restore calm. James opens the champagne, saying that it's bad luck to put off a celebration that's already planned. I don't know if it's true or if it's just nonsense, an excuse to drain the bottle. I drink my glass and go.

I'm a little late getting to work, and Damiano, the owner, gives me a threatening warning glance. What the fuck does he want? I've always been punctual. Halfway through the evening I tell Felice that I've decided to start praying. I'm amazed by his reaction: a long, warm embrace. He invites me to come to his house for lunch after prayers next Friday. According to him prayer is necessary to keep religious faith alive, especially in a foreign country. "God has shown you the right path, *allahu akbar!*" he says, sincerely moved. Me on the right path? Let's not go overboard.

SOFIA

It's almost impossible to keep any information secret in Viale Marconi. An example? Yesterday the architect asked for an explanation of the altercation the other day in the market. He told me that the racist imbecile has a nickname, the Beast, and that he's a dangerous felon. I told him what happened, but he didn't seem convinced by my version of the facts. Probably he's heard other ones. He was very insistent on knowing all the details. In other words, he subjected me to a detailed interrogation.

"What did that criminal say to you?"

"Nothing."

"What do you mean, nothing?"

"The usual racist things, like you're a mummy, go back to Afghanistan, you people are all terrorists, you come here to plant bombs."

"Did he insult you?"

"No."

"Did he hit you?"

"No! I stumbled and fell."

"Who was the man who intervened?"

"I don't know him."

"Arab or Italian?"

"Arab."

"How do you know?"

"Because he said something to me in Arabic."

"What did he say to you?"

"'Don't be scared.'"

"Now he absolutely has to be found."

"Why?"

"Because the Beast wants to kill him."

The Arab Marcello's life is in danger on account of me! He has to be warned immediately. I don't want to have the death of a guardian angel on my conscience.

My problem is that the architect uses the matter to gain other objectives. As usual it takes a while to get to the point.

"The Beast might also bother you again."

"What should I do? Stay shut up in the house?"

"No, I don't mean that. But I can go with you when you go out."

"You're practically asking me to become a recluse."

"What are you talking about?"

Ah no, architect, no thanks. You want to control me, find an outlet for your jealous husband's paranoia. This is a real trap, but I'm not going to fall into it. I'm not that stupid. And so? So what. I'll never agree to live closed up within four walls, gorging myself on stupid soap operas. I'm not the frightened little wife who needs her little husband to protect her. To hell with jealousy, fear, and the Beast!

Today is Friday, and I use the occasion to call my family. I hope to find my father at home: it would be nice to talk to him, since I haven't for a while. Little Cairo is crowded; many of the clients don't confine themselves to telephoning, like me, but stay to watch Madame Al Jazeera. The TV is useful for attracting clients and making them feel at home. Unfortunately a lot of them succumb to it. I don't know how they can sit for hours and hours watching the news of attacks, bombs, suicide bombers, wars, death. It's a daily media storm. A true doping of the mind and the memory. Poor immigrants, every day they absorb a huge amount of negativity, and are in danger of becoming sick, addicted.

Alas, it's a problem that I know close up. My happy husband Felice belongs to this unfortunate and cursed category. It's a dangerous dependency. And so? So what. I just hope that doctors and psychologists are doing something about finding a cure. In cases like this you need a drug, or am I wrong?

I glance around Little Cairo. Where is Akram alias secret polygamist? I don't see him. Better that way, better to avoid his questions. Even his looks can't be underestimated. He has an astonishing power—he can read your thoughts.

I don't see anything interesting to remark on. No sign of the Arab Marcello. Too bad, I'd like to warn him against the racist Beast.

I have a long wait, then booth No. 6 is free. I go in and dial the number of my house in Cairo. The line is busy. I wait a minute and try again. My heart starts pounding. It always happens like this—I get very emotional, as if I were to meet in person a loved one I hadn't seen in years. A serious male voice answers. I recognize it right away. After the usual greetings I say:

"Mamma told me that this year you're going together to make the pilgrimage to Mecca."

"Inshallah, we'll carry out the fifth duty of Islam."

"I'm really happy for you."

"Your mother and I are growing old. We've lived our life. We are only looking for *misk al khitam*, a happy ending."

"May God give you a long life, papa."

"Amen. We ask God to see our children and grandchildren happy."

"Inshallah, papa."

"Tell me about yourself. How are things going?"

"Thank God, we can't complain."

"You're right, my child. When we're healthy we must be content with what God gives us."

"That's right, papa."

"Will you come to Egypt this summer?"

"This year there is no *maktùb*, it will be the following summer, inshallah."

"Inshallah."

After the short chat with papa I talk to my mother. She brings me up to date on the preparations for the wedding of Layla, my little sister. Everything is going well, which is good, because a wedding celebration is very stressful. I got through it. I felt everything on my skin. You have to stay totally focused. First of all, don't forget to invite relatives and friends. Every inattention costs dearly. People are easily offended. A neglected invitation is enough to end a friendship that has lasted a lifetime. Then, you have to be able to endure a horrendous weariness. It takes entire weeks of rest to recover. In fact the best part of the honeymoon is that the newlyweds can finally relax.

After the phone call I make a quick trip to the market to do the shopping. I hope I won't run into the racist monster. I don't want to change my life because I'm afraid of another human being. As a Muslim I should fear only God the Almighty. I won't be intimidated. The market belongs to everyone, so I, too, have the right to come here when I like. Clear? I buy some vegetables. I don't need fruit, I stocked up yesterday. The Arab Marcello? He's not there.

I decide to go home without stopping at the Marconi library, because I have to make a big lunch. Today we're having a guest. My husband is very happy. He managed to persuade the Tunisian friend who works with him to go to prayers. And by guiding him onto the right path he receives a commission for good actions. It's a fruitful investment that leads directly to Paradise. In Islam there are many incentives to proselytize. For example, if someone teaches you the Koran, God will reward him every time you recite some verses. Same thing with prayer. And so? So what. My husband has turned into a proselytizer, a sort of Muslim evangelist. A fine outcome, isn't it? What satisfaction!

As a wife should I be happy or unhappy if my husband goes to paradise? The answer is very complicated. I'll try to simplify the question. So, Muslims are supposed to use their earthly life to gain eternal life. The principal goal of every believer is to earn this reward. You pray, you observe Ramadan, you make the pilgrimage to Mecca, and so on, for a precise reason: to get to paradise. But if you ask an observant Muslim why he is so attached to paradise, after some verbal acrobatics he will confess: houri! Here's what a good Muslim gets: beautiful women who remain virgins after every sexual encounter.

And so we reach the billion-euro question: what does a Muslim woman get if she has the good fortune to set foot in paradise? Houri? I don't think so, unless she's a lesbian. As far as I know lesbians and gays are excluded from the Muslim paradise. Do houri of the male sex exist? I doubt it. And so? So what. We have quite a problem to solve, don't we?

Now an important detail comes to mind. When we were in high school, a very bold friend asked the professor of Islamic studies this very question. The answer was simple: if a Muslim woman reaches Paradise she will find waiting for her the husband with whom she lived her earthly life. And this would be the reward? For heaven's sake! My classmates burst out: what if the woman wasn't happy with her husband in earthly life? Isn't Paradise supposed to be the place of happiness? So wouldn't it then become Hell for her? And what about the situation where the husband ends up in Hell because he was a murderer or a rapist: what will happen to the good wife? Also: what if the woman was unmarried or divorced, that is, without a husband?

The professor was dumbstruck. He had no answers to our questions. Probably he had never thought about it because he had never put himself in a woman's shoes. Anyway, I still don't understand what we're going to do (we women) if we win a place in Paradise. Here's why I worry about the religious future of my husband. With the life he leads, in which he follows the tiniest details of the dictates of Islam, it's likely he'll go to paradise. I, too, have all the necessary requirements so that I can hope not to end up in Hell. So will we find ourselves together in the other world? The truth is, this scenario doesn't excite me in the least. In other words, I find no incentives, you see?

My husband's Tunisian colleague is becoming an observant Muslim. The great event is set for today, when he makes his début at the Mosque of Peace. Too bad Al Jazeera wasn't informed in time—it will be a private ceremony, no TV cameras. Anyway, it doesn't matter, there will be a small celebration. For the occasion, the architect asked me to make lunch in honor of his friend. They'll come here after the Friday prayers.

I'm not too worried, I've got time to get everything ready. I'll cook some Egyptian dishes like *mulukhia* and baked chicken with rice. Aida is watching cartoons in the living room. She's very fond of Minnie, Mickey's eternal girlfriend.

Around two-thirty the architect arrives with his guest. He doesn't use his keys and so he rings the bell. I open the door and am stricken dumb. Total blackout! Earthquake!

"May I introduce brother Issa."

"Welcome."

"Thank you."

The Arab Marcello has a name: Issa. He is Tunisian, not Algerian. I must have been fooled a little by my Algerian friend Samira's accent. But I didn't take into account a crucial point: she has been married to a Tunisian for many years, and over time she's probably taken on her husband's accent. Accents change from one Arab country to another.

Thank God the architect is not aware of my agitation. During lunch very few words are exchanged. I act as if everything's normal and the Arab Marcello does the same. He is a little embarrassed, like me. And so? So what. I try not to look

DIVORCE ISLAMIC STYLE · 149

at him, but every so often our glances meet. I like his Tunisian accent. I think he'd look better with his hair slicked back, like John Travolta in *Grease*. Get rid of the mustache, it's really out of place. For Arabs hair continues to be the symbol of virility and paternal authority. I have nothing against it, but the harmony of the face as a whole has to take precedence.

Lunch proceeds smoothly. The guest eats eagerly. After tea he pays me a lot of compliments on my cooking. This gives me great pleasure. I wait for the architect and the Arab Marcello (I can't seem to call him Issa) to leave the house together to go to work. Then I rush to Samira's for an extraordinary summit meeting. The news of today is extremely important. A real scoop, as the journalists say, so it's useless to waste time in long introductions. I have to get right to the point. As soon as Samira opens the door I fire the first shot. And what a shot!

"The Arab Marcello came to lunch at my house!"

"Is this one of your dreams?"

"No, no dreams. It's pure reality, I swear."

"Are you kidding?"

Samira is right not to believe me. Even I can't convince myself that today's lunch really happened. The Arab Marcello was sitting opposite me for almost an hour. He ate what I cooked with my own hands. It's not a dream but, really, an exceptional event. It has to be said that *maktùb*, the will of God, has no limits.

I tell Samira the whole story from A to Z. I try not to omit a single detail, in order to allow her to make a complete diagnosis. Luckily my memory doesn't play tricks; in fact it's faithful and generous. After a long exposition of the facts I give my friend the floor.

"I don't have words, Sofia. This is really strange, I mean it doesn't seem true."

"Believe me, I didn't invent anything."

"Of course I believe you. You know, life is full of things we can't explain rationally."

Samira is completely right. I, too, have trouble believing it. Sometimes it's hard to tell where reality begins and ends.

A little later Giulia arrives to have her hair cut. She's smiling. What happened? Did she get a raise? Win the lottery? Has her companion finally decided to marry her?

"We're going to live in Australia."

"In Australia?"

"Yes, my companion got a job at the University of Sydney."

"When do you leave?"

"In three months."

Giulia is really happy. She tells me that her companion, a researcher in the field of new cell technologies, can't find a job in Italy, even though he's very good. Then she explains to me how the Italian university system functions, that is, like the Mafia: there are godfathers, like Don Corleone, and families that hold all the academic power. If you don't enter into the logic of the clan, you are excluded. At least three times she repeats, "There's no meritocracy in our country, only mediocrity."

Emigrate to Australia? Giulia isn't very worried about the place. She and her companion speak English well. And, with her degree in economics, she hopes to find a job easily. Maybe they'll open a business, and have more children. In other words, they're thinking big. Giulia wants to let it out, her heart is full.

"Sofia, Italy is like Monte Carlo, you can live here only if you already have money in your pocket. It's a country for tourists."

"No!"

"In Italy it's easy to become poor: just have a child."

"You're exaggerating."

"I'm an Italian and I love my country. But the truth is that there's no future here."

"There's no future here?"

"Yes, Sofia, you should leave Italy before it's too late."

"And where would we go?"

In Italy there's no future! Those words worry me a lot. I think automatically of my daughter, Aida, of her future. The Italians leave Italy to seek their fortune elsewhere. But we immigrants come here for the same reason. And so? So what. Something doesn't work. A country for tourists, not for workers. Giulia said, "Italy is like Monte Carlo." I'm curious about this comparison. There are casinos in Monte Carlo, where you gamble. I wonder: isn't immigration ultimately a form of gambling? Win everything or lose everything?

ISSA

The landlady, Teresa alias Vacation, arrives early in the morning for a surprise inspection. And by sheer coincidence she finds two illegal Egyptians sleeping in the kitchen. Immediately we start on a small digression. For Teresa the true illegal is not someone who doesn't have a residency permit but someone who doesn't pay rent. A tenant offered hospitality to some friend unbeknownst to her; it's very likely that she was tipped off. There's some truth to the hypothesis of the spy, of the informer in her pay; it's not bullshit or an urban legend. The lady does not show up like this as a courtesy call. In other words, she's not a person who goes to any trouble to be kind or to ask us, "How are you doing?" or "Boys, do you need anything?" As a good Sicilian I say, "You don't get something for nothing."

Teresa merely complains about the presence of the undeclared guests, insisting at length on the importance of trusting a relationship. Signora Vacation trusts us and we ought to trust her. She doesn't mention the threat of increasing the number of beds. Maybe it's not the moment to attack. Some of the tenants take advantage of this opportunity to bring up the problem of the hot-water heater, and she promises to take care of it as soon as possible. The real reason for her unexpected visit is the case of Saber. There's been a real dust-up, or, rather, a tragedy. The cause? Simona! Who? Simona Barberini. Yes, her.

So let's go in chronological order, starting from the beginning, that is, from the other day. My Egyptian friend returns home from work late. He's very tired, so he changes and goes to bed. As usual, he wants to give a good night kiss to his Simona (yes indeed, to the photo of Simona Barberini hanging next to his bed). Unfortunately it's not there. Someone has taken it, stolen it, seized it! Saber makes a scene. He refuses to go to bed without getting to the bottom of the situation. He starts shouting "Who stole my Simona?" "Who took my Simona?" "Give me back my Simona!" and "I waaaant Simonaaaa!" He was like the madman in Fellini's *Amarcord* when he climbs up a tree and refuses to come down, shouting, "I want a wooooooman!"

Compared with Fellini's madman, Saber has a precise and sensible request: he doesn't want a generic woman, but a woman with a first name and last name. It's not a small thing.

In Arabic Saber means "patient." In reality this man could have all the qualities in the world, but patience isn't among them. So, when one of the tenants points out, "This Simona isn't your wife!" he gets furious and says, "Simona is more than a wife, get it?" someone else tries to make him see reason: "Don't be foolish, Saber. Remember you're illegal and you can be expelled." And he, weeping, "I'm not afraid of the bolice."

The "abduction of Simona" took an unexpected turn when a dispute broke out between the observant tenants, on the one hand, and the non-practicing, on the other, after which Saber openly accused the former of stealing the photo. Finally, as a challenge, the Egyptian placed an ultimatum: "If you don't give back my Simona within twenty-four hours, I swear I'll hang up the calendar that shows her naked, and not in the bedroom but in the kitchen, the bathroom, everywhere! Then we'll see what you do!" A real declaration of war.

Saber has become the knight of individual liberty, the enemy of fundamentalism, the last bastion of freedom of expression on Viale Marconi. To listen to him speak you'd think he was a great enlightenment intellectual. I was struck by some of his arguments, like "Today it was boor Simona's turn, tomorrow it will be someone else's," "Sooner or later they'll force us to have a beard down to our neck, and wear the loose shirt, and marry a woman in a burka." Or: "Fucking shit, this house is a nest of Taliban."

Anyway, the fundamental basis of his reasoning is a liberal principle: everyone has the right to do what he likes provided it doesn't irritate his neighbor. Since Simona (O.K., the little photograph of Simona Barberini) didn't bother anyone, who- ever stole it has committed a serious crime. But evidently the presence of Simona (alas, the last trace of a woman in the whole apartment!) disturbed the peace and the slumbers of one of the tenants.

Finally, around dawn and after many attempts at mediation, we managed to calm him down. He slept like a child exhausted after playing all day.

The business will not stop here but will surely have conse- quences. The question to pose is the following: will the power of the observant in this household come to a halt? In other words: will the non-practicing have the balls to bring home wine and women? Only time will tell.

My priorities are different from Saber's. For me bringing my mission to a conclusion is more important than anything else. So I follow Judas's order and decide to start my prayers today, Friday, the Muslim holy day. The rumor has spread among the tenants that I'm about to cross over into the caste of the observant. Saber is rather amazed, but I relieved him by telling him that I consider religion a strictly private matter. In other words, I'm not against Simona Barberini's presence in the house. Anyway, I accept the good wishes and congratula- tions of my new observant companions. I wait to see the first concrete advantage of this choice: saying goodbye to the line for the bathroom.

Islam doesn't fool around with hygiene. To pray it's essential to be clean. Many observant believers, including my fellow-tenants, take advantage of the Friday prayers to have a shower. In order not to rouse suspicions I do, too, even though heating the water in the kitchen and then carrying it to the bathroom is a real pain in the neck.

In the late morning I say goodbye to Mohammed, who is leaving for Morocco. The signs of melancholy and depression in his face have vanished. He has rediscovered his smile and his taste for witty remarks and, especially, jokes. He tells me he can't wait to embrace his children (about his wife not a word). Before he got his new residency permit, he lived like a hostage. He couldn't leave Italy without running the risk of being stopped at immigration on his return and sent back to his own country.

Before leaving to go to the airport Mohammed takes me aside and says in a low voice, "I've noticed that you go to Little Cairo every day."

"Right, I go to call my family in Tunisia."

"Be careful!"

"Of what?"

"Don't talk too much on the telephone."

Right afterward he explains to me that in recent years many Muslim immigrants have been arrested on account of telephone calls, and thrown in jail to await trial. And he tells me the story of a fellow-Moroccan, a resident of a city in the North, who was arrested because he said this phrase to a friend on the telephone: "I intend to open an Islamic *màjzara*, inshallah." Some interpreter, out of incompetence, perhaps, or in bad faith, translated the word *màjzara* as "slaughter" rather than as "butcher shop"! The investigators had no doubts: the Moroccan immigrant was an Islamic terrorist who was planning an Islamic-style slaughter. The poor man, blameless and the father of a family, spent a long period in jail.

I leave the house and stop first in the park in Piazza Meucci, then at the Marconi library: no sign of the beautiful girl in the veil. I go on to Little Cairo hoping to see her there, but not a trace. Akram, too, is absent. Maybe he's preparing for Friday prayers. In his place there's a smart young kid, on the threshold of adolescence. I find out that he's Akram's son; his name is Galal. Today Little Cairo is full of people. Waiting for a booth to be free I listen to him talking with two Italians. I'm impressed by the way he speaks: in a very pure Roman dialect, just like the street kids played by Carlo Verdone. Curious, I ask him some questions.

"Bravo! You speak the Roman dialect perfectly. How did you learn it?"

"Naturally. I was born in Rome. My friends are almost all Romans."

"How many languages do you speak?"

"Arabic, Italian, Roman, and a little English."

"Bravo!"

"Normal."

"You're really lucky."

"Me lucky? I wouldn't say so."

"Why?"

"In Rome they call me the Egyptian and in Cairo the Italian."

Neither fish nor fowl, Galal means. Like being everywhere and nowhere. Bum deal! His isn't an isolated case; it's a problem for an entire generation of immigrants' children, who were born in Italy or who came here as children. There are almost a million waiting to become Italian citizens.

I call Tunis. My "mamma" answers. We talk for ten minutes. Subject of the conversation is my marriage. "Son, you're not a child anymore. You have to settle down." I let her talk— I don't have much to say on the subject. Every so often I interrupt with some nonsense like "You're right, mamma," or "Inshallah, I'll get married soon, mamma." Anyway, at the end

I give her carte blanche in the search for her future daughter-in-law. Better not to waste time. You have to be practical.

Around one o'clock I head for the Mosque of Peace. It takes a few minutes to get there. I'm sort of excited. It's the first time I've gone into a mosque to pray. During my trips to Arab countries I've visited a lot of mosques. Exactly: I went to visit, not to pray.

From the outside the place resembles a garage rather than a mosque. Let's say it's just a place of worship: the real mosque is a whole other thing. I take off my shoes and enter with my right foot, as tradition requires. I see the imam, Signor Halal, and I go to say hello to him.

"*Assalamu aleikum*, Imam Zaki."

"*Aleikum salam*, brother Issa. Welcome to the house of God."

"Thank you."

"Prayer is essential for us immigrants. May God bless you."

"Amen."

I sit on the floor and wait for Felice. After a while Ali, the convert I met the other day as I was leaving Little Cairo, comes over. Judas told me a few things about his past: before converting to Islam he was a militant on the extreme left, a hard-line Communist who would not accept compromises. He may have been connected to the Red Brigades, but no evidence was ever found. He's probably the ideologue of the cell, or at least has an important role in the new organization. Does Operation Little Cairo provide a chance to make him pay his outstanding account: does he have blood on his hands? Certainly if he is guilty it wouldn't be right to let him get away with it. Anyone who does wrong should pay, always.

We start talking about the situation of Muslims in Italy. Now Ali is a lawyer who does volunteer work for the foreigners. He explains that the Italian constitution guarantees freedom of worship, but adds that in reality Muslims are heavily discriminated against. Although Islam is still considered a religion of immigrants, in fact there are more than ten thousand Italian citizens who are followers of the Koran, and they all have the sacrosanct right to have decent places of worship. A couple of times he cites Articles III and XIX of the Constitution; the first is the one that concerns the equality of all citizens before the law, the second sanctions freedom of worship.

Then he tells me that this place used to be a warehouse. It's always very damp, hot in summer and freezing in winter. He adds that it's very difficult to get permission to open a mosque, and complains about certain Italian political leaders and their extreme provocations of Muslims.

Ali isn't sparing in his criticisms of the Italian government, which wants to adopt a law like the Patriot Act—the law that Bush passed after the attacks of September 11th to combat terrorism, which gave much greater power to the security services and reduced individual freedoms. Then he offers a comparison between the current campaign of alarmism and the strategy of tension carried out by the services during the seventies and eighties, Italy's "years of lead."

"When I was at university I was drawn to the ideas of the Brigades."

"Brigades?"

"The Red Brigades, you know who they are?"

"No."

"They're the ones who in 1978 kidnapped and killed Aldo Moro, then the leader of the Christian Democrats."

I'm astonished by his confession. I wonder: why is Ali admitting this particular? Shouldn't he keep his ties to the Red Brigades hidden?

The convert continues to tell me, briefly, his story. At university he came in contact with a group of Brigade members, but he was never involved in bloodshed. At the time, he was certain that violence was the only means of changing and improving the world; now he admits that he was wrong.

"Power is corrupt to the marrow and tends to militarize dissent in order to sweep it away. Today I believe that nonviolence is a more effective tool. I always urge my brothers in Islam not to fall into the trap of terrorism."

At this point Felice arrives. He greets me and sits down next to me. Imam Zaki starts the sermon. The theme is peace in Islam. After the sermon, the faithful rise, and then begin a series of movements punctuated by ritual formulas uttered by the imam. I imitate them mechanically, like a robot.

When the prayer is over I go, as promised, with Felice to his house. It's near Little Cairo. I buy an apple cake. The elevator stops at the fourth floor. Felice rings the bell and who should open it but . . . It's her . . . the beautiful woman in the veil. She—she is Felice's wife . . . I see the child hiding behind her and calling her mamma. It's her daughter.

I'm overwhelmed with emotion, or, rather, I'm literally stunned. The food is good, but I can't fully taste the chicken and rice. I feel ill at ease, out of place.

Before going to work I stop at Via Nazionale to see Captain Judas and bring him up to date on the situation. I find him sitting in the living room intently reading a document.

"Tell me, Tunisian, how did your first day as an observant Muslim in the mosque go?"

"Fine. The imam devoted his sermon to . . . "

"To peace in Islam."

"How do you know?"

"It's written in this report, Tunisian."

"Ah . . . so I'm not the only spy in this operation."

"What a cheeky bastard, your imam, he talks about peace while they're plotting attacks. Anything else?"

"After prayers I went to Felice's for lunch. I met his daughter Aida and his wife . . . "

"Safia, Sofia to her friends, a very beautiful woman. Don't you think?"

"Yes, you're right."

"Isn't she the woman you defended at the market?"

"Yes, it's her."

"But didn't you say you didn't know her?"

"It's true—I only really met her today."

"I see. Listen, you want to see her naked?"

"Are you kidding?"

"No, I'm serious."

Judas takes some DVDs out of a drawer. As he inserts the first one in the portable disk player he tells me that they bugged Felice's apartment and also planted tiny telecameras in it. But what does it mean? That my colleague is part of the second cell, that he is in fact the head? Who would have imagined?

The first film begins: Sofia is in the living room with the child. Felice arrives. They talk about the trip to Egypt. He complains about the cost, the tickets are too expensive, all the gifts for the relatives . . . Sofia tries to convince her husband to let her work to help with the expenses, but he objects. They begin to argue. The little girl starts crying.

Second film: Felice is sitting in the living room and watching a program on Al Jazeera. Sofia arrives, in her nightgown, without the veil. She's like a different woman. It's her hair that makes the difference. She's beautiful. The two are talking about the fight at the market. Felice asks her a lot of questions, Sofia says she doesn't know me.

"What are they saying, Tunisian?"

"Problems of couples."

"They're not talking about attacks?"

"No."

We watch more DVDs; the arguments are very frequent. Then comes the hardcore part. Felice and Sofia are nude in bed and they're making love. I am speechless, Judas comes out with vulgar comments. What's happening to me? I couldn't be jealous?

"Your friend is hopeless in bed, but she's a knockout. Look at that body, the tits, the ass. Look, Tunisian!"

"That's enough!"

"Wait, between one sigh and the next they'll say something about the attacks!"

"Shit! I completely forgot that I have to go to work!"

"It's not the end of the world. Call the restaurant and pretend you're sick. You know what I say? Tonight let's have a nice break. I'll take you out."

"Where?"

"Surprise. How long since you've been laid?"

"I've lost count."

"You like dark or blond?"

"Dark."

"Arab looks?"

"O.K."

"With a veil, maybe?"

"Fuck you!"

I have the evening free. I take off my immigrant clothes and put on the dark-blue suit that I left in the apartment on Via Nazionale when I moved to Viale Marconi. Judas takes me to a villa on the Via Cassia. The party has already begun. There are a lot of girls, all beautiful and all vivacious. Judas introduces me to a dark-haired girl and says, "*Ya Tunisi, hadhi al shabba al Arabia, halal aleik!* Tunisian, this beautiful Arab girl is yours!"

Shit, this dickhead knows Arabic! I'm impressed by his pronunciation. It's almost perfect. My instinct is to ask if he really speaks it, but I don't. I'm completely enchanted by the beauty of the girl. We sit on a couch, finally alone, and start talking. She tells me a few things, like that she is Lebanese and works in a travel agency. I have no intention of coming on as the Arabist. I want to forget my shit habit of showing off by asking questions meant to impress, like: you say you're

Lebanese, let's see, are you Maronite Christian or Muslim? If you're Muslim are you Sunni or Shiite? If you're Shiite, are you close to Hezbollah or the movement of Amel? In other words, the obsession to prove that I know the other well, rather, to always have to astonish him. That's what the work of the Arabist consists of. A crappy occupation, precisely!

Late in the evening Antar and James, alias Starsky & Hutch, join us. The C.I.A. agent is already drunk. Antar puts on a CD of Arab music and stars dancing Egyptian style. My mind is very tired, I just want to forget everything and relax. Yes, relaaaax. I'm drinking vodka. I've turned into into a raging bull. I'm incredibly excited. I find myself in bed with the Lebanese girl, we're naked, caught in an embrace. After that, total blackout. I don't remember anything, not a thing.

The next day I wake up in a big bedroom, completely naked. I'm not alone: there's a surprise. Next to me is a young black guy, also unclothed. I decide not to wake him. What happened? Where did the others go? And the beautiful Lebanese girl, what happened to her? Captain Judas has also disappeared. I get dressed and leave in a hurry.

SOFIA

It all happens quickly, like a strong, sudden storm. I'm sleeping. The architect wakes me abruptly. I open my eyes with a sensation of fear. My first thought goes to Aida. The second thought is an earthquake. I continue to have nightmares because of the terrible quake that hit Cairo in 1992, where more than five hundred people died. My architect is agitated, angry, he's barking like a wild dog. What's happening? It takes me a few seconds to emerge from sleep and return to reality. His voice invades my ears aggressively.

"Who does this money belong to? I found it hidden behind the sofa."

"It's mine."

"How did you get it?"

"I can't tell you."

"What?"

I get out of bed. I glance at the alarm clock on the night table: it's three-fifteen in the morning. Satan be damned! Damn him, too. Why doesn't he let me sleep? Why doesn't he leave me in peace and spend the rest of the night with Al Jazeera, his real mistress? I go into the bathroom and wash my face. I can't close the door: Felice follows me like a shadow and starts shouting

"How did you get this money?"

"I don't want to tell you."

"You must tell me immediately."

The bathroom is next to Aida's room. In order not to wake

her I go back to the bedroom. I say to myself that if we have to discuss, or, rather, fight, it's better to do it here. I sit on the right side of the bed, my side. My head is spinning, but I resist and try to soothe the waters. I choose the diplomacy route, maybe it will get me somewhere.

"Please, it's very late. It's not the moment to discuss it."

"I don't give a damn. I asked you a question and I want an answer."

"You're tired, why don't you come to bed?"

"Do you want to provoke me?"

"No. I'm just asking you to rest."

"Don't make fun of me!"

"All right. But don't shout, the child is sleeping."

"I will not calm down until I know how you got this damn money."

"All right, I'll explain it all, but later."

"No, I want the truth now."

Damn the devil! The architect wants the truth. Telling the truth is a serious thing, it requires premises, parentheses, and notes. The question is very complicated. And so? So what. If I tell Felice *my* truth, will he believe me? If I tell him that the money he discovered comes exclusively from my secret career as a hairdresser and is to be used to help my sister Zeineb have an operation, will he comprehend it? Will he understand me? I'm sure he won't. Try explaining to him that the operation is to repair the damage done by circumcision. He can't understand. These are difficult things to relate, to justify, to explain . . . . It's likely that he has found out about my clandestine work. Further confirmation that you can't hide anything on Viale Marconi. Secrets don't exist. Anyway, I refuse to speak. It's better to maintain silence, at least right now. I try to gain time, then we'll see. Unfortunately he won't let go.

"I want to know the truth about the money."

"Please, let's sleep now. We're tired."

"I don't want to sleep. I want to know the truth."

"I'm repeating for the last time. I don't feel like talking *now*."

"You're not the one who decides when the moment is. I'm the man in this house."

"But I'm not your slave."

"You're not a slave, you're a *sharmùta!* Only a *sharmùta* earns money without working."

It's the first time I've heard this word come out of his mouth. It's worse than a bullet in the heart. Wounds heal, because they affect the body, but certain words can wound forever, because they go right to the depths of the soul. *Sharmùta*, whore! *Sharmùta* to me! How dare you!

This I can't let go. You will pay for this, my dear Felice. I swear it. I can't remain silent, I have to react. Even patience has a limit, as Om Kalthoum says. I get up from the bed and now we're face to face.

"You're right. But if I'm a *sharmùta*, as you say, then you are the husband of a *sharmùta*."

"Shut that mouth."

A hard slap knocks me to the floor. My nose is bleeding. I get up and stare at him in defiance. Now I have nothing to lose. I move to the attack, the final assault.

"If you're really a man, divorce me now."

"Shut up or I'll kill you."

"You're a coward."

"*Anti tàliq*, you are divorced!"

Anti tàliq! Anti tàliq! Anti tàliq! I repeat these two words over and over to myself. I start crying. The third divorce is final. I feel that something in me is changing. There are knots that are loosening, thoughts and memories that rise to the surface.

I say to myself, "Freedom! Finally I'm free." Hooray for the third divorce! Who says that divorce has to be the end of me? A death sentence? Why can't it be a beginning instead? I want to decide for myself. Why should I be afraid? The future will be better, inshallah. I'll be able to live as I like. I'll find my way. God is always merciful, he closes one door and opens many others.

But . . . what will become of me? I don't have a real job . . . and my child? My poor Aida?

I persist in convincing myself that divorce is not a tragedy but an absolution. Liberation from a life without dreams and without love. I think of my family—it won't be easy to explain to them what happened. But it's not my fault. I'll have to call and tell them. I want the news to be official. I'm not looking for compromise, or reconciliation. I want to put the word "end" on this marriage. I'm inclined to run the risk. Better divorced than unhappily married. Why go on like this?

After an hour or so my ex-husband calms down and goes to sleep. I wait for morning in the living room, accompanied by tears. Around eight I take Aida and go to Samira's. As soon as she sees me she can tell that something serious has happened. I can't hide my emotions. She reads everything in my face. I explain what happened without omitting the slightest detail. I can't stop crying. She tries to soothe me with gentle words and embraces. And above all she refrains from asking that terrible question that makes you feel alone and desperate: "What are you going to do now?" The only answer I'd have is "I don't know!"

Samira helps me get my thoughts in order. I need an emergency plan, a way of getting out of this awful crisis. First, my position should be very clear from the start: no reconciliation. This time, the divorce is final. Second, it has to be made public. If I could, I would even let Al Jazeera know. I don't care at all about the scandal. It wasn't my fault. I'm the injured party. I'm the divorced one, aren't I, or am I wrong? And so? So what. I mustn't be ashamed. Third, I don't want to stay under the same roof as the architect anymore. Clear?

"Sofia, you can come and stay with me."

"But what about your husband?"

"He left for Tunis yesterday, he'll be gone for two weeks."

After a couple of hours the architect shows up. Obviously he knows where to find me. Samira leaves us alone in the living room, taking Aida to the other room. The architect starts weeping like a baby. This is déjà vu! It's like a scene from a very boring soap opera. The title could be *Divorce Islamic Style 3*. He repeats like a parrot, "I'm sorry."

I tell him that I'm coming with Aida to stay with Samira, but he won't agree to that. After some back and forth he suggests that he should leave the house. I consent. It's better that way—I won't disturb my friend.

At lunchtime I go to Little Cairo to call my parents. I feel like a messenger bearing news of the death of a close relative. After three attempts mamma answers. When she asks, "How are you, daughter?" I burst into tears. I shouldn't, but it's stronger than I am. It takes a little time to collect myself and tell her everything. My mother interrupts me only to sigh, saying, "*Ya msibti!* What a catastrophe!" I try to calm her, but it's not easy. For a woman like her the word "divorce" is worse than the plague. I'm sure she'll soon discover that times have changed. And then I live in Rome, not Cairo. I'm far away from the social pressures that divorcées and unmarried women are subject to in Egypt.

Finally she asks the feared question.

"What are you going do now, my dear?"

"I don't know."

"Come to Cairo, your family's here. You're not an orphan."

"I have to think about it."

"You can't stay there alone, without a husband."

Go back to Egypt? That's out of the question, especially right now. And then if I go back to Egypt I won't be able to protect my daughter from circumcision. Anyway, I have to be diplomatic in order not to become the one who is in the wrong. I can't afford the luxury of losing my family's support.

I've got to stand firm. If I go back to Egypt I'll never leave. Yes, I have to be firm and gain time. I know that God Almighty won't abandon me and will help me find a way out.

When I go to pay I find Akram waiting for me like a hungry wolf. Does he want to talk to me? It seems he does. He takes me aside. Don't tell me he already knows the latest developments in the soap opera *Divorce Islamic Style in Viale Marconi!*

"I heard about your misfortune, madame."

"Misfortune?"

"Yes, the third divorce. It's *maktùb*."

"Of course, it's *maktùb*."

"I wanted to tell you that we're like a family. You can count on me."

"Thank you, *hagg* Akram."

"Don't mention it."

Satan be damned! What do I have to put up with! A soap opera based on a true story. The worst of the worst of the Egyptian, Brazilian, Mexican, and Turkish together. How terrible it is to play the role of a divorced woman, rather, a woman dealing with the third and final divorce!

In the afternoon I go home. I see that the architect has taken his black suitcase. I glance at the bathroom, there's no sign of the electric razor. So he's gone. A couple of hours later, I hear someone knocking at the door. I open it and who should I see before me? Aisha the convert, alias Signora Haram. The last time I threw her out of the house. Now she's back. Why didn't she ring the outside bell?

"I heard about the tragedy, sister."

"What tragedy?"

"The third divorce."

"Ah yes."

"We are sisters in Islam and we have to help each other in difficult moments."

Thank you."

"A Muslim woman can't live without a husband, sister."

"Why not?"

"Because that's the way it is."

"There are Muslim widows and divorced women who are happy and satisfied."

"What are you saying, sister? You are very young."

Maybe Aisha came to get revenge, or to feel out the terrain, to propose me to her husband. Did he send her? If I'm not wrong the butcher has two wives: one regular and the other secret. So there are still two free places. Aisha is a hundred percent submissive to him. If he told her to throw herself in the Tiber or the Nile she would do it without a moment's hesitation. In the end, as she's leaving, she looks me in the eyes and says, "If you need help you can count on me." She seems sincere, very sincere.

I call Giulia and Dorina. I'll recount this new episode in the soap opera *Divorce Islamic Style in Viale Marconi*. They show up in twenty minutes. They are fond of me. I summarize the facts yet again. As we Arabs say, "*Iaada ifada,* repetition is beneficial." Dorina takes the opportunity to vent and take a weight off her mind: "Men are bastards, period. They're bullies. Castrate them all. They're all shits!"

Giulia, on the other hand, argues against marriage as an institution. She summarizes her theory with the maxim "There would be no divorce without marriage." Then she urges me to regain my freedom as a woman. "Sofia, now you should throw out those male traditions and take off that damn veil."

But I don't want to reopen that question. Women's freedom can't be reduced to a matter of clothes. It's more complicated. What about those girls who dance half-naked on TV or appear on calendars without veils? Are they truly liberated women?

Two days after divorce No. 3 the architect comes home, early. You can see he hasn't slept. He's sad, in fact very sad. But I can't do anything. We sit in the living room. I tell Aida to go and play in her room. I try to listen to him out of pure politeness because I have no desire to talk or to hear his apologies. After a short silence he looks at me and says:

"We have to find a way out."

"A way out?"

"Yes."

"I don't see one."

"Every problem has a solution."

"I must remind you that the third divorce is final."

"Even the third divorce has a solution."

"In what sense?"

"We'll look for a *muhàllil*."

"A *muhàllil*? Are you joking?"

"No, I'm serious."

My ex-husband isn't joking at all. Scenes come to mind from the play in which the comic Adel Imam plays the role of the *muhàllil*. Irony of fate! My ex-husband explains to me that the *muhàllil* is in conformity with Islam. This word derives from *halal* and means literally: "make something legal." However, I'm not going to be influenced by his apologies. According to his plan I should marry another Muslim and then divorce him. That way we could go back to being man and wife. I pretend not to understand, I want to see how far his delusion will go. I start with a question:

"If I understand you, I have to marry a Muslim only on paper? Is that right?"

"No, I'm an observant Muslim. I don't want to make fun of my religion."

"What do you mean?"

"The marriage has to be consummated."

I can't believe my ears. He's talking about a real marriage.

In other words, I have to marry a man, obviously a Muslim, and go to bed with him. Clear? He considers me goods to sell and buy back.

I try to maintain my self-control. I want to hear his ridiculous speech to the end. My ex-husband notes an important consideration about the figure of the *muhàllil*. Through the *muhàllil* God punishes the husband who has uttered the divorce formula three times. Imagining his wife in someone else's bed, even just for a night, is a great punishment. The poor wife (in this case that means me) has no say in the matter.

My patience is wearing thin, but I hold out. Soon I'll tell him to go to hell, not right away. There's no hurry. I can't deny that I'm rather amused. I have to play the game, his game. I ask another question:

"Where are you going to find this *muhallil*?"

"I've already found him."

"Really?"

"Yes."

"Don't tell me it's Akram, the owner of Little Cairo."

"No, I don't trust him."

"Yes, they say he has three wives. I could be the fourth. So it would close the circle."

"No, it's not Akram."

"Then it must be the imam butcher, Signor Haram."

"No, not him. Anyway it's better if he's not Egyptian."

"Oh, I see, he's not Egyptian. Will you tell me who it is?"

"My friend Issa."

"The Tunisian?"

"Yes. If you agree I'll talk to him right away."

Issa the Tunisian, alias the Arab Marcello. This is certainly news. Now *Divorce Islamic Style in Viale Marconi* has surpassed all the Egyptian, Mexican, Brazilian, and Turkish soap operas put together.

Here's a proposal that interests me! I ought to accept immediately, without asking my girlfriends for advice. Maybe it's a sign of *maktùb*.

I like the Arab Marcello a lot. I suppose I'm a little in love with him, as Samira says. In the end, after thinking it over a bit, I tell the architect that I accept, generally speaking, his candidate.

In the afternoon I decide to go to Little Cairo to call my family. I'd like to relieve their minds. As soon as I arrive I see the Arab Marcello, watching Al Jazeera. Now we have to get serious. I go over and ask him straight out to meet me at the Marconi library. It will be more tranquil, far from Akram's surveillance.

He arrives in ten minutes. I like to get right to the point. And so? So what. He just has to say if he agrees or not about the marriage. A very simple question, or am I wrong? Thank God, the architect has already talked to him, so I can be spared a rendition of the idiotic scene of the divorced woman looking for a new husband, her savior.

"Will you agree?"

"You mean to get married and divorce right afterward, so you can marry Felice again?"

"No, I don't want to marry him again. Our marriage is over forever."

"Felice is my friend, I can't betray him."

"Why talk about betrayal? It's all *halal*. I am now divorced and I can marry someone else, as long as he's a Muslim, and you are. Islam is clear on this point."

"Sofia . . . I . . . can't."

"Why not?"

"I can't."

"Because you don't want a divorced woman, with a child, besides?"

"It's not that."

"Then you want a virgin, like the suicide bombers!"

"What are you talking about?"

"Then why?"

The Arab Marcello is in love with me. You can read it in his eyes. I feel it when he takes my hand. But he is very troubled. I have a feeling that he has a secret. What can it be? Maybe it's something he can't confess. He reminds me of Marcello Mastroianni in *Bell'Antonio*, when he hides his impotence from his wife in every possible way. Or in *A Special Day*, when he finally abandons his flirtation with Sophia Loren because he's a homosexual.

Arab Marcello, what are you hiding from me?

It's possible that he's afraid of the responsibilities of marriage. In other words, I'm also the mother of a daughter. I know Arabs very well, because I'm an Arab. I know they're fixated on virginity. And I, alas, I'm not a virgin, what can I do about it? Well, I could always become one again, if it turned out to be indispensable. A small grant to the cosmetic surgeon would be sufficient.

I feel that this guy really does love me, but . . . but he's afraid. Of what? Of whom? I trust my feminine intuition. I'm sure he's hiding something from me.

Arab Marcello, why don't you tell me the truth?

ISSA

aber wakes me at seven in the morning. He whispers, in order not to disturb our sleeping companions—Felice is looking for me, he's waiting at the door. What does he want? They've discovered everything and are going to do me in? Has the moment of truth arrived, time for action?

I get up feeling a bit dopey, put on my slippers and leave the room. I see Felice leaning against the door. Instinctively I look at his hands. Luckily he's not holding a gun or, worse, a knife. Just at this moment I think of the last sequences in the video showing poor Nick Berg, the young American kidnapped in Iraq in 2004, having his throat cut.

"Hello, Felice."

"Hello, Issa, I'm sorry to bother you."

"Everything all right?"

"I'd like to ask a huge favor."

"What?"

"Not here, let's go out."

I ask for ten minutes to go to the toilet, wash my face, and change. It takes even less time because the bathroom is free. The place is quite peaceful this morning.

I join Felice, who in the meantime has gone downstairs and is waiting at the entrance of the buildng. I suggest that we go have breakfast at the café, but he doesn't want to, he's in too much of a hurry. Without wasting any more time I ask, "What's the matter, Felice? You look tired."

"I'm in trouble—I've made an unforgivable mistake."

"What did you do?"

"I divorced my wife for the third time. So now she's not my wife anymore."

Felice tells me the whole story, in all its details. He reveals for the first time some details of his marriage. He admits, for example, that Sofia doesn't love him as much as he loves her, and that she doesn't want to have more children. Felice would like to have a boy, to name after his father, who died a couple of years ago. I'm touched to see him weeping in despair. He admits that he's responsible. He keeps repeating, "Jealousy is a terrible disease." He's very worried about his daughter's future. He explains to me that the third divorce is final. Now he can't even touch Sofia, it's *haram*. If he wants her back as his wife, she has to marry another man, obviously a Muslim, and then divorce him. Then, and only then, can Felice remarry her. What acrobatics! A true religious somersault.

"Issa, you're the only one who can help me out of this nightmare."

"Me? how?"

"You have to marry my wife."

"What? Marry your wife?"

"You're a respectable person, Issa, and I trust you. I've persuaded her, she'll do it."

Felice immediately moves on to the practical aspects. The marriage has to be consummated. Translated into Italian: Sofia and I have to make love, like a married couple. I don't dare ask how many times we have to do it. We men are obsessed with quantity, women prefer quality. What bullshit clichés are rushing into my mind now!

I'm getting a headache, without my morning coffee. This is certainly a remarkable situation, completely out of the ordinary. It doesn't happen every day that someone, an observant Muslim, besides, asks you to marry his wife and go to bed with her. It seems more like something for swingers. Could there be

Islamic swinging or swinging Islamic style? Enough, don't be ridiculous.

Felice uses all the weapons at his disposal to try and persuade me, and even resorts to a couple of quotations from the Prophet, one on friendship and the other on solidarity. He also comes out with a verse from the Koran, but I don't understand the connection with what we're saying. I prefer to skip over it. I feel sympathy for him, goodness knows, but how can I do what he asks?

Still, I go along with the game, I listen patiently to his arguments. He wants to settle things right away to cut off any gossip. I doubt that he'll succeed—news like this spreads in the blink of an eye. That bullshit privacy doesn't exist on Viale Marconi. The story could end up on Al Jazeera: MUSLIM IMMIGRANT SEEKS HUSBAND FOR OWN WIFE! News like that would overshadow even the appearance of Osama bin Laden in a world exclusive on Al Jazeera. Scandal on a global level.

We part, finally, with an emotional embrace, leaving the "negotiations" open. After all, we'll see each other this afternoon at work.

I immediately go to the café for an espresso to get rid of my headache. Sofia and I as husband and wife! Who could have imagined it? I feel something for her, it's pointless to deny it. I think of her constantly. It would be great to marry her and disappear into the void. Far away from Viale Marconi, Judas, Felice, and everyone. Only her and me, and, if she wants, her daughter as well. That's no problem, I'll be a father to her. Have Sofia beside me, look into her eyes, touch her, kiss her. Am I awake or dreaming?

Stop this raving. I have to reason with my head, I can't just listen to the heart. Ah, the head, it still hurts. One coffee is not enough. I order another. Run away with Sofia. That's a good plan. Where could we go? Sicily? Tunisia? We'd have to cover our tracks, the way secret agents do when they decide to end their career and change their life. Cut the cord and go forward, without turning back. Marry Sofia. Be the husband of Sofia. Have the children of Sofia. Shit, I'm delirious.

The truth is that this business is a real black hole, there is no hope of finding a way out. So why the self-delusion? I would have to tell her everything, reveal that I'm not a Tunisian Muslim immigrant but an Italian informer. A spy. I'm sure she wouldn't understand and would never forgive me. I imagine the scene:

"Sofia, I'd like to tell you a secret."

"What, Issa?"

"My name isn't Issa but Christian, and I'm not a Muslim immigrant from Tunisia."

"Really? Then who are you?"

"I'm Sicilian."

"Really?"

"Yes, and I'm a spy for the Italian secret service."

"What?"

"I've even seen you naked while you make love with Felice."

"You're a piece of shit. I never want to see you again. Fuck off!"

I leave the bar and decide to take a walk. I get almost all the way to Viale Trastevere. Walking helps me relax a little.

Then I retrace my steps and head for Little Cairo. I go in. I don't see Akram, in his place there's a very tall kid. He's probably Egyptian, too. Today I have neither the intention nor the desire to call my "Tunisian family." I don't want to hear anything else, I've already had my daily fill of news. I just watch Al Jazeera. It's showing a repeat of a program of political analysis: three guests in a studio in London and a fourth connected by video in New York. They're talking about a new fashion in Arab regimes: leaders handing over power to their own children. Even though the subject is interesting, even entertaining, I can't manage to concentrate. Around and around, and I always end up with the image of Sofia. It's a real obsession.

What the fuck should I do? Inform Captain Judas about it or leave him in the dark? Agree to marry her, whatever the cost? A grand love story like this doesn't happen every day. My mental jerk-off doesn't last long. I'm distracted by the shouting of one of the participants on the talk show, an Arab from the opposition in exile in the British capital. "A country," he cries, "cannot be considered property, like a house at the sea or in the mountains, to leave as an inheritance to one's children. We have hit bottom, we can't go any further. We Arabs are pitiful in the eyes of all the peoples of the world. We have to. . ." I don't have time to hear the whole litany because who do I see emerging from one of the booths? Sofia!

She comes over.

"Hello."

"Hello."

"I have to talk to you."

"O.K."

"I'll expect you at the Marconi library in ten minutes."

I pretend I'm still following the television debate, but now my mind is elsewhere. I leave Little Cairo after a couple of minutes. Staying in one place makes me more anxious. Better to walk to get rid of some of the tension. I cross the market and reach the Marconi library punctually. I go up to the first floor. She's waiting for me, and wastes no time with preliminaries.

"My ex-husband told you about the marriage?"

"Yes."

"And you've agreed?"

I ask myself, why are women always in a hurry? This question I don't want to hear. At least, not now. It's a real trap. I can't answer. Life can't be white or black. Shit, isn't there gray? Or not?

The truth is that I have a great fear of losing her, so I try to gain time. I take advantage of her desire to unburden herself. So I also hear her version of the events. It's not different from

Felice's, except for one detail. He thinks there's still hope of mending the breach, while for her there's no way: the third divorce is irrevocable. I'm moved when I see her tears. I feel like hugging her, but I can't. I simply place my hand on hers. It's the first time I've touched her. A charge of electricity runs through my whole body.

"So you agree to the marriage?"

I have no answer. Sofia is very patient, she wants to soothe me. She has definite ideas about the future, *our* future. I needn't worry about the financial aspect, despite my precarious situation. *L'occhi chini e 'a panza vacanti*: eyes full and stomach empty. She says that she'll get work as a hairdresser (it's the first time I've heard of a hairdresser who wears a veil in Italy), it shouldn't be a problem, because she's very good. She already has some regular clients. She has a plan to set up on her own.

We make a date for the next day, same place and same time, to exchange news.

In the early afternoon I get a phone call from Captain Judas. He wants to see me urgently. Not at operation headquarters in Via Nazionale but in a café near Piazza della Radio. Why all this hurry? He'll blow my cover if he keeps this up!

It doesn't take me long to reach the place of the appointment. He's sitting in a corner, but one from which he can see everything. He's in a good mood.

"Hello, Tunisian."

"What the fuck is going on, captain? Why did you tell me to come here? What's happened to all the precautions?"

"Sit down, we have to drink a toast."

"The occasion?"

"Your mission is completed. If you like, you can return to Sicily today."

"What do you mean?"

"We've identified the two suicide bombers."

"And who might they be?"

"Your friend Felice and his better half."

"Sofia?"

"The very one. What luck! It's the first instance in the West of a woman suicide bomber."

"Are you sure?"

"Very sure."

Triumphantly, Judas tells me that while we're there drinking our toast the police are arresting all the members of the two cells: Akram, Imam Zaki alias Signor Halal, Ali the convert, and, obviously, the couple Felice and Sofia (I wonder: didn't he hear the story of the third divorce?). Tomorrow morning there will be a big press conference revealing the behind-the-scenes details of Operation Little Cairo. High U.S. and Egyptian officials are arriving in Rome. We'll be well rewarded: for him almost surely a promotion to the rank of commander, for me money and good opportunities for work in Italy and abroad. Then he tells me that the discovery of the identity of the two suicide bombers was possible thanks to the decoding of an event that took place the other day: Felice and Sofia spread the news of their divorce, and that was the coded message to take action. Because if they divorce now, that is, before blowing themselves up, they can be married again in Paradise.

This story makes no sense. It doesn't stand up. It doesn't convince me at all. I can't remain silent.

"I'm really sorry, but I don't see any evidence."

"What bullshit is that, Tunisian. We have tons of proof, more than enough to fuck them all. In Italy in recent years we've arrested quite a number of Muslim immigrants on charges of terrorism, on the basis of circumstantial evidence, never or almost never real proof. I'm telling you, there's no problem: we're sure that the terrorists of Viale Marconi are really the plotters."

"Oh yes? Then you must have also found the explosives."

"No, but we've taken steps."

"In what sense?"

"Tonight we planted a moderate amount of TNT in their fine mosque."

"So you want to get them!"

"Tunisian, are you with us or with them?"

"I'm with the truth."

"I repeat, they are not innocent people, understand? But if we didn't find the explosives they would immediately relax and we would look like shit. The explosive material is the bait to force them to confess everything."

"I'm sorry, but I don't agree with those methods."

"I don't give a shit about your opinion. You do only what I tell you, otherwise it's your affair."

"Are you threatening me?"

"I've told you many times that we are at war. You have to decide if you're with me or against me. I will not allow you to ruin the entire operation."

"I'm not afraid of you. I'm sure they don't have a damn thing to do with it."

"My dear Tunisian, you force me to be more persuasive. You remember that night you spent with the Lebanese girl? The next morning, when you woke up, you found yourself next to a handsome black guy, completely naked. Right? Obviously you don't remember shit about what happened that night. Is that right? Well, I have a very compromising DVD. You understand me? I could send a copy as a gift to your relatives and all your acquaintances, or simply put it on the Web. What do you say?"

"I say you're a real son of a bitch."

"Or we can insert you in the group of terrorists. It's easy to construct a story for you. For example, you could have been recruited by Al Qaeda during one of your frequent trips to the Arab world. So you would be not only a terrorist but also a traitor. The press would immediately rename you 'the Italian Taliban.'"

"You nasty son of a bitch."

"Believe me, I can destroy you and your family in many

182 · AMARA LAKHOUS

ways and with minimum effort. And, as we say among ourselves, when a man has his back to the wall he thinks only of
saving his own ass!"

"Bastard!"

"You can't pull out now, you and I are in the same boat: one
for all and all for one. Remember that we're at war. You've got
to decide which side you're on."

"Fucking son of a bitch."

"Maybe you've forgotten Italian. Would you like to speak in
Arabic?"

I'm astonished. Judas speaks perfect Arabic! His accent is
Middle Eastern; it could be Lebanese, Palestinian, or even
Syrian. He tells me briefly his history with the Arab language,
and about long periods in Beirut and Damascus. He spent
many years in the Arab world as a secret agent.

"You see, Tunisian, you've been dishonest with me. You've
kept a few little things hidden from me . . . for example, that
you went and fell in love with a suicide bomber! Do you realize that?"

Judas knew about the thing with Sofia from the start. I was
followed and spied on twenty-four hours a day.

I don't feel like saying anything, maybe because I have
nothing to say. Better to listen.

"Tunisian, I repeat for the last time: are you with me or
against me?"

"Bastard."

"Are you with me or not?"

"Yes."

"Bravo, Tunisian! You've made the right choice and you
won't regret it. Now you can read the short document that I've
prepared for my superiors. I'd like to get your opinion."

I take the page, which is printed on letterhead. This time
nothing is blacked out.

Subject: Operation "Christian Stopped at Viale Marconi."

I first heard of Christian Mazzari alias Issa from a colleague who was stationed in an Arab country. He told me that there was a Sicilian kid who spoke Arabic better than the Arabs. I was curious and wanted to meet him. I followed him for months both in Sicily and on his trips to the Arab world. I was able to study him from close up, discovering both his strong points and his weaknesses.

Christian Mazzari has some characteristics that make him interesting for us.

First, he has a Mediterranean physiognomy. Second, he speaks Arabic as if it were his mother tongue. Third, he is very bright. Fourth, he has a good memory.

Operation Little Cairo was a test, but also, above all, good training. The purpose was to flush out an Islamic terrorist cell in the area of Viale Marconi, obviously nonexistent. Christian showed a great capacity for adapting, sharing a house with eleven persons and working as a dishwasher and then an assistant pizza maker. He proved that he could manage a double life.

We can therefore conclude that the training went well. The mastery on the part of Christian alias Issa of the Arab language is a trump card that we can use not only on Italian soil but on delicate missions abroad. Now it all depends on him. We await with confidence his response to the offer to work for us.

Rome, 24 June 2005

I finish reading the report with astonishment. I feel like a person who is suffocating and needs air. I have to reverse roles: this time I want to ask Captain Judas the questions.

"So Operation Little Cairo was all staged?"

"Staged? Nooo. You read it: it was a test, a training exercise."

"A sort of *Candid Camera*, a *Truman Show* Italian style!"

"Let's say you did a tryout at a high level, at the international level. On some things you did well, like the capacity to adapt to rather hard conditions. On others less, like the test of women."

"The test of women?"

"Tunisian, if you decide to do our job you have to learn a vital rule: never love women, only fuck them."

"In other words, if I understand you clearly, there's no trace of terrorists or suicide bombers in Viale Marconi? Is that right?"

"Yes, Tunisian. At least, as far as I know."

"So no arrests and no press conference."

"No, I don't think so."

"And James, the C.I.A. agent?"

"He's a colleague, one of us."

"And Antar?"

"The same. They, like you, passed the test as well. The four of us would make a good team. I'm tired of seeing so many incompetent people around. Ours is a difficult job."

"And the photos of Akram at Mecca?"

"Nothing to do with terrorism. Akram is just a big womanizer. A real whorer Islamic style."

"Judas, I think I've already told you: you're a real bastard!"

"I know. That's why I'm called Judas and not Issa, like you. So, what do you say? You want to work with me?"

"I have to think about it."

"They all say that before they accept. But you'd better be quick, Tunisian. We're in the middle of the War on Terror."

"War on terror? Don't be ridiculous!"

ABOUT THE AUTHOR

Amara Lakhous was born in Algiers in 1970. He has a degree in philosophy from the University of Algiers and another in cultural anthropology from the University la Sapienza, Rome. *Clash of Civilizations Over an Elevator in Piazza Vittorio* (Europa Editions, 2008) was awarded Italy's prestigious Flaiano Prize and was described by the *Seattle Times* as a "wonderfully offbeat novel." Lakhous lives in Italy.